A bold and powerful anthology offering poetry and prose from a diversity of new and established women writers, *It's All Connected* ripples and blazes across a universe of topics, a galaxy of tones. Deftly constructed, moving from ancient myth to present day narratives, from pre-history to future worlds, this book arrives as an elegant feminist fanfare.

—Carmel Bird

A feisty, vigorous and eclectic volume; feminism is alive and well as a creative force …

—Gail Jones

A wonderfully rich and diverse expression of full throttle womanhood.

—Amanda Lohrey

IT'S ALL CONNECTED

Feminist Fiction and Poetry

Edited by Pauline Hopkins

We respectfully acknowledge the wisdom of Aboriginal and Torres Strait Islander peoples and their custodianship of the lands and waterways. Spinifex offices are located on Djiru, Bunurong, Wadawurrung, Eora, and Noongar Country.

We also acknowledge the many women throughout history who have fought for women's freedom and the freedom of lesbians, often at the cost of their lives.

First published by Spinifex Press, 2022

Spinifex Press Pty Ltd
PO Box 5270, North Geelong, VIC 3215, Australia
PO Box 105, Mission Beach, QLD 4852, Australia
women@spinifexpress.com.au
www.spinifexpress.com.au

Edited by Pauline Hopkins
In-house editing by Susan Hawthorne
Cover design by Deb Snibson
Typesetting by Helen Christie, Blue Wren Books
Typeset in Adobe Garamond
Printed by McPherson's Printing Group

 A catalogue record for this book is available from the National Library of Australia

ISBN: 9781925950564 (paperback)
ISBN: 9781925950571 (ebook)

Contents

Unfolding: An Introduction

PAULINE HOPKINS

> Every second, stories unfold all over the place. Some are unfolding as they happen, some haven't happened yet, some never will—and that turns out to be the story. There are stories nested inside stories, with more nested inside them, out past infinity. And they keep unfolding, continuously, simultaneously, skeins living along the same yarn.
>
> —Robin Morgan, *Parallax* (Spinifex Press, 2019)

In 2021, as Spinifex Press marked its 30th year as a dedicated feminist press, the non-fiction anthology *Not Dead Yet: Feminism, Passion and Women's Liberation* was published to recognise the contribution of women over 70 to the feminist cause.

This year, as Spinifex Press continues into its fourth decade of publishing women's stories, we wanted to celebrate fiction and poetry that have been such a crucial part of the publishing house since its inception.

In these pages you will find an eclectic collection of women's voices—some who have been part of the Spinifex list before, and others who are published here as Spinifex writers for the first time. They are all women with stories to tell, real or imagined, remembered or forgotten. But what these poems and stories have in common is an essential truth, each capturing the heartfelt emotions and ideas of authors who have generously dared to share something of themselves on the page.

I have had the great joy and challenge of bringing this collection together and have been moved and thrilled at the quality of the writing, the creativity of the pieces and the skill and talent of these women. I hope that readers encountering a poet or short story writer here for the first time will be encouraged to explore their other works.

Some pieces are poignant; others are funny or tragic. Some seethe with anger, others swell with joy. Some are manifestly Australian in flavour, others distinctly international; some are universal, drawing on myths and stories many of us know. All are relatable, challenging and thoughtful.

Contributor Diane Bell is a renowned anthropologist who has written with passion and courage on Indigenous land rights, native title, law reform, women's rights, violence against women, religion and the environment. Spinifex Press has published a number of her books including *Ngarrindjeri Wurruwarrin: A World That Is, Was, and Will Be*, as well as her novel *Evil*, in which we were introduced to feminist sleuth Dee Scrutari, who makes a welcome return in the title story of the collection. This story captures many of the themes that are reflected in this anthology—the environment and natural resources, journey and discovery, relationships between people and animals, land and colonisation, politics and power, belonging and alienation, time past and present, words. *The stories, the families, the country, the River.* It is all connected.

In a short introduction is impossible to mention every amazing writer who has been included in this anthology, but I do need to make special mention of Jordie Albiston, who died tragically early in 2022 as this book was being compiled. She received the Patrick White Literary Award in 2019 for her outstanding contribution to Australian literature and it was Spinifex Press which published her first poetry collection *Nervous Arcs*. We are fortunate to be able to include three of her poems here in print for the first time.

For me, to be able to work for a dedicated feminist press that cares about women's stories is a dream come true. I invite you to enjoy and experience these expertly crafted stories and poems, written with precision and attention. It has been a privilege to edit this anthology and collaborate with women who care as much about the written word as I do.

Pauline Hopkins
Melbourne, October 2022

Agamemnon's Return from Troy

as told by Clytemnestra

JENA WOODHOUSE

I shuddered when I saw her eyes—
their ghastly shadows and their fires;
they'd seen more than a girl like her
should ever see. Apparently, we'd heard,
she had the gift of prophecy, though she was also
cursed by this, by what she couldn't *help* but see.

Then I saw my husband's eyes, lascivious,
regarding her—not me, his wife whom he'd
not seen for ten long years—but her, his whore!
My vengeance hardened to a blade, although
I led them both inside with words reserved
for guests, and had my handmaidens make up
their bed. They'd never get to warm those silks
and linens, I would see to that, but let them
relish the pretence, enjoy the banquet
and the bath, drink their fill of wine
as dark as wounds that stiffen in their gore,
before his fleshy bulk prepared
to launch itself on her slight form.

Her witch eyes seemed to read me
through the tangle of her wild coiffure;
her slatternly apparel seemed to magnetise
King Agamemnon: like his gaze, his hands
kept straying to her countenance, her breasts,
her belly's curve, where some would-be
usurper coiled in foetal rest.
She did not flicker in response, but nor did she
rebuff his touch. The warrior had lost his wits,
but not the urge to thrust.

I'd waited ten years for this day, this night
of triumph, his return. I'd not waited alone,
it's true, but then, had he? I'll wager not.
How dare he flaunt his lust before me!
How could I so foolishly expect
better of Agamemnon, who'd thought
nothing of our daughter, no more than he would
of any beast the priests select for slaughter—
gluttonous for auguries, to speed
Mycenae's vengeful fleet—

What do my own shame and guilt contribute
to this tidal wave of bile that rises up within
and will not be suppressed? Ah, woe to Iphigeneia,
and woe to me, to Clytemnestra, craven mother
that I was, to not slay Agamemnon then!
Woe to you, Cassandra, pretty witch who so
beguiles old men! You'll not see out the night,
my dear, but meanwhile, Welcome to Mycenae!
(said with all the dignity a woman spurned,
a queen, can feign). Come in! We've been
expecting you! Your valedictory feast awaits!

Deranged at seeing still more gore,
that witch-child, Agamemnon's whore,
turned to me, expectant for the blade
that mingled blood with blood—
the marriage she had come to consummate,
imposter at our gate—Agamemnon's
souvenir of Troy, a prophetess and slut:
Clytemnestra, she began, my thrust making
her gasp for breath, *Beware your children,*
Clytemnestra! Shun Orestes and Elektra!

Was this her final oracle? I took it as
a Parthian shot, a viper's venom from her lips
writhing in the throes of death, Troy's
prophetess, once-lovely priestess,
in the arms of Thanatos.

Ulyssea

SUSAN HAWTHORNE

What is the velocity of a falling body?

A body falling through space sensing neither the relative time nor the relative motion of its fall.

How long does a body falling into a seizure take to fall?

Which is the time?
Which is the space?

The time is now and long ago. It is a time when the world is slipping from one shape to another. There is great confusion and shape shifting is taken to mean that only some have genuine lives worth celebrating. This is a tale about Ulyssea. A woman, who in her old age has been heard to say, "What mattered was not the past, but now. In my ten thousand years of existence, I have never seen anything so strange."

It was different when she was young. As a young woman, Ulyssea sat not at the feet of her elders but beside them, listening to the stories they had to tell of a world where plants grew naturally; where animals came and went and some of them told their stories in languages which only women could understand. Ulyssea heard wonderful tales of the forests and the seas, even of the bounty of deserts.

Ulyssea heard the stories of creation, and there were many stories. Her favourite was the one about how the world was compared to the way a butterfly emerges from its pupae; in which clay is compared to the awkward and some say ugly caterpillar. It is said that after the passage of time—a time sometimes long, sometimes short—a transformation takes place and the worm, the caterpillar, the unformed clay is transformed into a great beauty. This butterfly in some stories has red wings or gold or green, but Ulyssea sees before her eyes a butterfly with bright blue wings, wings the colour of the sky.

In her youth Ulyssea dreamt of places she might visit, see the worlds of others, eat foods unknown to her, hear the words of languages whose tongue she searches for in her mouth. Whatever world they speak about, it is its beauty, its ability to regenerate, to recycle and to transform that lies behind the tales.

If a body is senseless to the motion, the time, the space, the pull of gravity as she falls, can she be a sentient body?

If a body only notices that she has fallen (now face down on the ground) that it happened some time before this moment (her eyes open to her position but not to any memory) how can she know she has fallen? That time itself has been seized? That memory has not encoded the moment or actualisation of the fall? What then?

If memory has for a moment (or for several unquantifiable moments) been erased, scrubbed clean by the fall through time, through space, what proof has she that she exists?

Echidna was born underground. She is prickly this one, and in her adulthood, she took off for the caves. She was sick of everyone insulting her.

"Monster," they said, over and over again.

She said, "I'll give you monster," and she proceeded to give birth to all sorts of weird and wonderful creatures. There are dogs and snakes, goats and lions, birds and dragons.

But does Echidna exist? She's gone underground, no one wants to know her, she's been cancelled over and over again.

Sounds familiar, sounds just like the strangeness old Ulyssea was talking about.

Ten thousand years. A prehistory in which many fabulous things might happen. In which monsters might truly roam the world. Think of slippery Scylla, barking Cerberus and Chimera; a wild sow from the village of Crommyon and many-headed Hydra who could replace any head she lost. And there are the triplets, the Gorgons who are the granddaughters of Echidna: Medusa, Stheno and Euryale.

The rain is pelting down. She knew it would come because the butterflies had been floating around the garden for the last few days. Ulysses butterflies. Bright blue. They like it best if you walk through the garden in blue clothes. Then they'll sit on your shoulder.

Ulyssea likes to float, to glide between times. In her mind she stands on the edge of a cliff, looking north across the sea where the Amazons once roamed. She sees them in their tight-fitting pants, almost like dancers' tights. She has heard that it was Amazons who invented trousers. They needed them to prevent chafing when riding. As with so much else, men came along and took over that garment.

When men wear dresses, they shoot up the hierarchy as popes or mullahs, rabbis or monks. The world is a strange place.

Heading along the Black Sea coast, she is behind the wheel, following the road's hairpins. It turns back on itself multiple times, sometimes climbing, sometimes easing down the cliffside. She pulls up in a small town with rows of cafés looking out over the sea. Red and white gingham cloths covered in transparent plastic.

The coffee is sweet, the baklava more so.

But that was ten years ago and now she must rely on memory, on photos, on the books she reads so avidly.

> Only later when she says, "What happened?" (assuming something did) can she call on her existence. But when she fell, sensing none of the things essential to conscious existence, did she exist as anything more than an object falling?

> She can know only that she has fallen through space into another time but only as an object. At the moment of non-existence, she cannot be a subject (except that she is subject to the laws of gravity and the continuous flow of space/time).

Falling through time is nothing new for her. She also specialises in falling through space. Or rather, she used to. She says, "I have experienced earth's shudder. The one that runs through you and before you know it you are down for the count."

When the sun comes out the air heats. The humidity like a steaming pot. She decides that it's time to rig the trapeze. It's been a long time, but she has a sudden burst of energy. She goes to the box under the desk and hauls out the gear. But she's forgotten how to string it up to the high metal beam. Photos. Finding the right one that will have a picture of the top bit, the part that no one ever thinks to photograph. Eventually she finds one and the penny drops.

She tosses the rope over the bar, finds the heavy slings, and attaches the ropes with a couple of carabiners and some good strong knots to keep it all in place.

She's up and on to the bar. So long she's waited to get back up here. Next, she puts up the *tissu* which some people call silks, and she climbs. She can still do it. It's five years since she's been on her gear, after they moved everything from one house to another.

Ulyssea remembers a particular performance they had planned, although it never happened. It was to be called *Monster* after Robin Morgan's poem. Hilda and Helen had organised the meeting to devise the ideas and shape.

It had been Hilda's idea to create a long-lost world of women, she wanted to have a character Helen in the show, but a different Helen than the one she had written about in Egypt. This Helen had neither run off with a beautiful man, nor escaped a war-torn city rushing across the sea to the southern edge of the Mediterranean. This Helen had taken off on her own (well not totally, she had her helpers, women who knew about boats and horses, cooking and weaving). That's the thing about myth, the big names always have the unnamed behind them. But this is a contemporary story and so the women who were hanging out together did have a range of skills. Both Hilda and Helen were excellent storytellers and astronomers. Hilda's father had been an astronomer and Helen too was tutored in star lore.

Hilda begins, "Who do we want to include in this performance? Some names, please."

"Echidna," says Erica. "She has such a bad name as the mother of all monsters. She took off for the caves because she was sick of being insulted by these young upstarts who thought they could rule the world."

"Wasn't she a snake as well as a woman?" That was Rosanna speaking. No one owned up to being the parents of Echidna, too much shame. But Echidna's children were cool about their mother's reputation. What is interesting about both Echidna and her children is that they are a mix of different creatures. "So," says Rosanna, "lots of opportunity for dress-ups."

"I want to be an aerial Scylla," says Ulyssea, always with her head in the clouds. "I can slide down the silks and outsmart anyone who approaches me. "

Kore, who is much more grounded says, "I'll base anyone who'll have me. I'll take on the persona of that sow. Run around that old village and carry performers from one part of the stage to another."

"We'll do a three-woman trapeze act," call out Mary, Genevieve and Kate. "Starting on the ground, we'll go up and up and unfurl our wings at the top."

The echo of these words is like a prose of rain. Falling in great blasts of wind or in a drizzle of depression. Which words do we want? The ones that mean something. Or a fabrication of reality?

"Words," mutters Ulyssea to herself, "mean a lot. When I say woman, I mean a female body who has grown up in the culture of women, sisters, mothers, aunts, grandmothers as well as long-term friends who mean more to so many women than their intimate male partners. For us lesbians best friends and intimate partners are mostly one and the same."

She has no one to talk to so she continues speaking out loud to herself, "It's not about a feeling, it's about reality. Even if I have a feeling that I am related to that monster Echidna, it won't change that I have a human body. Not the body of a snake, not a multi-headed snake. You can hate me as much as you like, but this body is that of a female, a woman, an adult human female."

At the moment of non-existence during the fall, she (like any particle) could move along one of two paths a tendency towards non-existence (death) in which case the subjectless state would have persisted or she could resonate towards a tendency to exist (which she did) and move towards the possibility of subjectivity.

She leaves a frail trace of light burning brighter as consciousness returns to her eyes.

She lives.

now he dreams the Sirens silent—

after Benjamin, after Kafka[1]

MARION MAY CAMPBELL

now he dreams the Sirens silent
within the roar of his blood
within the trough the winds carve for his boat
mast-tied   beeswax-plugged

he keeps no company
his fiancée's letters all dissolved
right to the remnant F
he knows the oceanic terror of music

that ineluctable drowning
he must forgo seduction forgo the crew
to be plunged
into untold silence

and so the Sirens swing him by
their nipples scorching suns
their claws excoriating
the cliff's blue limestone

1   Walter Benjamin, 'Franz Kafka', *Illuminations: Essays and Reflections*, trans. Harry Zohn; ed. & intro. Hannah Arendt; pref. Leon Wieseltier, New York: Schocken Books, 1969, pp. 117–118.
Franz Kafka, 'The Sirens', *Parables and Paradoxes*, Bilingual Edition in German and English, New York: Schokken Books, 1974, p. 93.

their throats open beyond all earthly operatics
carry a key he'd written F
when she still clung to the initial
and one day, beyond the window-blind city

there will be a door
that will open up for you
the Sirens now sign in his dream
only in the radiance of seascape's elimination

only in her evanescence
will you lend her the right key
if we had been singing when we saw you
cruise by ecstatic

we would've mouthed sadly
nothing works anymore baby
history has stuttered you
between us cliff-hangers

and the tone-deaf sailors
there's no code no key
now that you loom   bitter ghost
beyond all Penelopes

The End of the Mountains

AVIVA XUE

Why didn't he kill me?

In the early morning, when the heavy purple glow spread itself over the valley, I was lying on the grass, wet and cold, staring at the sky whose blue turned lighter and lighter, and that's the first thing that came into my mind.

Thinking of 'me', my consciousness reluctantly gathered to my own body, immediately I sensed the burning aches all over. So again, I set my mind free to the sky, where the color was still growing lighter. My physical pain declined from a clear-cut sharp image to a mosaic of dots. I threw it behind as dirty clothes to be washed sooner or later, but not today.

But he came back, humming a tune in a language I couldn't understand. My heart shrank and my mind couldn't fly any more. It seemed that he fed his horse first and then sat boiling something beside me.

I vaguely remembered that I had been fed a bowl of thick porridge or something, completely unable to recall its taste. I glimpsed the smoke. Whatever was being boiled in the pot must be warm, I guessed. A desire for the warmth was immediately aroused in me, which he obviously sensed, for he grinned at me triumphantly and stirred the contents in a more leisurely way.

Not until I was showing desperation did he slowly fill the bowl and put it before my lips.

Seeing the equivocal smile on his dark face, I was puzzled. But the hot steam and refreshing smell of crops had risen to my nose, so I lowered my head, drinking the porridge hastily. The hot thick liquid infused life back into my exhausted body, assuring me one more time that I was still alive, with the more and more intense pains as the best evidence. We're either imprisoned in life or in death. Except this side and the other side, we can go nowhere. Moreover, the pass in between appears and disappears randomly, completely out of our control.

I was still imprisoned in life, by him.

Why didn't he kill me?

I thought he would definitely kill me. The reason was quite obvious: here, between us, he was the dictator. But outside the mountains, the world was run by another set of laws beyond his control, where I could send him for punishment.

The third day he led me to this mountainous land as my guide, he assaulted me. When the lurking perils that I had sensed all the way turned into a real danger, I was slow to react. Terror came from all directions and besieged me. But at first, I still managed to get rid of him and ran as fast as I could, but not faster than his horse. He caught me and struck me to the ground with his fists. Breathless, I climbed up and was beaten down, once and yet again. At that time, I thought I was done; he would kill me afterwards for sure. When he stripped me and penetrated my body, my arms and legs were stiff and I couldn't make a tiny move. I couldn't even feel my body at that moment. But this never made things easier. I lost consciousness. When I woke up, I found I was alive.

"It's about time." He was speaking to me seriously, observing the sky. "You must get yourself ready. We will set off when I come back."

I was still lying on the ground when he came back with his horse. He was irritated and lashed the whip in the air, making sharp strident noises, and shouted at me violently.

I cried, totally captured by panic. Trembling, I scrambled to my feet and climbed on to the back of the horse with all my strength as I was ordered. Then we set off.

The mountains were so high, so thick. The road was like a long thin snake, running zigzag cunningly. We moved on, but seemed never to progress any farther forward.

I on the back of the horse wept, hardly breathing. He, once set off, returned to normal. Yeah, normal. He strolled at a leisurely pace, never impatient about the endless road, as if everything fell within his control.

"Fine, fine, take it easy," he said, with a grass stem in his mouth. "We could climb over the pass today."

His words were so normal, even his manners amiable, as if he had never lost his temper this morning; as if he had never raped me yesterday; as if it was me that was unreasonable and knew nothing, and I should be ashamed of myself.

For one second, I did feel embarrassed and stopped weeping. Tears dried on my face. Then tiredness enveloped me again; all my senses and consciousness blurred and slowed, floating into the air, rising over the mountain road with his humming. Everything was usual and normal.

There was something stonily heavy in my heart, declaring to me that nothing was usual and normal. I shouldn't be here. I was full of regret. Where was the end of the mire?

In the stifling regret remained only one gleam of hope: we would get out sooner or later, and revenge would greet me outside, if I wasn't dead by then.

Time ran at uniform speed, smoothly, steadily and indifferently, as I stared at one silhouette of mountain after another. He said something strange to me, about somewhere faraway and the rocks under his feet, but I couldn't understand, which triggered his anger again. He whipped the grasses besides the road.

I asked, trembling, "How far is the end of the mountains?"

He pointed to the front, "Not far."

I looked forward confusingly, and my sight was soon blocked by a high mountain at a near distance. Beyond this one? My heart shivered, like a flame over a lighted candle.

I realized he had turned back to look at my face, observing and considering something. I got flurried and lowered my head. Had he seen through my plan? I didn't know. But in a few minutes, he ordered suddenly, "Stop!"

The horse was always at his call; it stopped in no time. Then he commanded at me, "Get down!"

With even my teeth trembling, I responded, "Why not move on?"

He stepped forward and pulled me down from the horse. I fell to the stony track head down; I ached to the bone.

He ordered, "Go collect firewood and cook!"

I was sure he did this deliberately to prolong the journey. Both of us knew that his power was limited to the mountainous land, and something outside could empower me. Once out, I would kill him, as I swore to do.

But he wouldn't let it happen. Had he decided when to kill me? He was standing there, fondling the neck of the horse. I couldn't read his mind.

I walked up along the slope, staggering and collecting the white dry twigs scattered on the ground. I collected terror and sorrow and hatred, and pressed them against my breast, tightly.

Wood collected, fire set and porridge ready, he gobbled and I barely swallowed any. Then he was busy on this or that, not mentioning anything about setting off. I dared not mention it and pretended not to care. Each time he came near the horse, the flame of hope sparked in my heart. But once again, he fondled the horse's head and turned away. I fell into sheer desperation, but soon enough we were on track again.

This time the journey was even more longsome. For each step, I told myself I was on the way out. He turned back now and then, looking at me sarcastically, which made me alarmed and grow uncertain about my belief. Isn't there really an end?

When we came to a narrow abrupt slope, he let me walk. I began puffing after several steps, but I struggled forward. He walked fast, and the horse, too. Without my burden, the animal was happily running forward, flicking his tail. They turned back, laughing at me. He said, "You're too slow! Do you want to be out?"

I had no energy to worry about his plan. Even if I died the next second, let me take a look, let me reach the end of the mountains.

I reached the top, step by step, after falling three times and getting scratched on my face and arms. My lungs hardened in fire and heart tightened with yearning, but when I looked down, what I saw was a plateau grassland, and beyond it there were still mountains, endless mountains.

Mountains after mountains.

I sat on the ground, weak and limp, and realized that I had been fooled. I turned to him full of hatred. At that moment, he sat relaxing, tidying his shoes, and the horse was feeding nearby. He didn't even bother to raise his head or give me a glance. Suddenly, he burst out laughing, openly amused by my desperate attempt.

I thought I should pretend that I hadn't hoped for anything better and that nothing was beyond my expectation. But the heavy loss and confusion dominated me; I couldn't help bursting into tears. I constrained my fear and shouted at him, "You lied to me! You lied to me!"

He raised his head with surprise. Obviously he didn't expect I would cry out. He thought I would, like before, keep silent and let it pass, then he could secretly feel pleased and proud. But now, he had to respond to the questioning. Language was not his strength. "It's generally …" He halted, and eventually gave up. Instead, he shouted and cursed as he led the horse, and commanded me to move on. I was suffocated by his anger and gave in as I was used to. He was satisfied immediately, and we moved on.

Yesterday I regretted being here. But today I finally realized that it's not me who had chosen to be here; it's that I AM here. Of course, it doesn't mean I have lived with him since I was born. What I mean is that my fate is tied up here or there. So, I either came here to be with him, or went to another place to be with another similar horse keeper. There are no other possibilities.

The sudden realization sheds a new light on these mountains, clouds, tall trees, and grasslands, which were no longer as strange as I had believed. Weren't they all that I had? This thought made me desperate but peaceful. On horseback, my sight caressed every pebble and every leaf, with neither joy nor sorrow.

My manner made him uneasy. He murmured once and again, "I did change a road … I must do it, must, you understand? Climb over this one and we get there!"

I seemed not to be listening. Actually, I didn't hear him clearly. I didn't care about his promise, because no matter how hard he promised, the end could not be found behind this mountain, or another one; and no matter how hard he lied, this road would come to an end eventually.

"Admit it," I said. "You do not know the road."

He was astonished for a second, and then shouted angrily, "I do not know? So, you know? How dare you …"

I did not respond. He pulled me down from the back of the horse again. He and his horse soon took the lead far ahead. He stepped forward and whistled at me triumphantly. I didn't bother to raise my head, walking slowly while counting the pebbles under my feet. The next time he shouted and laughed at me, I straightaway sat down and only set off again after getting my breath back. After several rounds, he ran to me and pushed me on to the horse, saying I was wasting time.

He cursed me endlessly. I was neither listening nor reacting. He suddenly stopped talking, so the whole world fell quiet. Hardly had I smelled the conspiracy behind the silence when the horse suddenly rushed ahead. I screamed, and he laughed.

The horse stopped abruptly at a whistle coming from behind me. I was thrown forward from the saddle, hitting the ground and I heard the cracking of my bones. I rolled and screamed on the ground in great pain.

He ran near and looked down at me, saying, "Bad … it's bad." But I could see from his eyes that he was trying to restrain his joy. He collected firewood, set a fire and boiled porridge. He gave me the porridge to eat, just like the morning after he raped me. At that time, I could feel the warmth, but now I just felt it was too coarse. Everything I touched turned painful. Eventually it made the whole world painful.

The next morning, glancing at me, he asserted, "Bad, it's really bad. But you did it to yourself … And I need to take care of you."

"How?" I asked.

He replied after a long-time hesitation. "We move on. We will arrive after climbing this mountain."

I swallowed all the porridge and lay down to gather my strength. When he stepped near, I threw my body at him and grasped his broadsword from his waist. I headed directly to the horse. He chased me, shouting and threatening. Seeing me put the sword against the horse's neck, he stopped and stared at me in terror, crying, "Madwoman! Madwoman!"

I swung the blade to the horse's neck. The neck was cut open and the horse neighed tragically and kneeled to the ground. The horse blood was spilled all over my body.

My broken bones grew and my wounds healed.

The two of us continued staggering on the mountainous road. He was speechless and I was speechless. Several times we reached forks in the road, and no matter which one I chose, he would frown at me, implying that I had made a terrible, stupid decision that he could never agree to. But each time, he would follow.

Mountains after mountains. He withered, but I became more and more energetic. Someone had told me that mountains would not stretch forever, and this road would come to an end.

As to how I would take revenge against him? I don't care, for I know there's an end and I will arrive.

Suburu

JORDIE ALBISTON

barn   gate   sign   tomb   squares flash by & circles
too   the sun sadly buried   a badly
hung moon   how I love the geometry
of silence   sometimes I stop to swig down
a sight or lap at a wound or forget

a someone at home   then I go on   how
lonely is a-lone   is it a woman
spinning a car right round the earth beneath
a stellified sky   is it only what?
three hundred miles?   put your heart back like a

clock   I gape at the moon while you're safe in
some room with more stars than a flag or a
Suburu   still   dark   fog   bare   how the gum's
stubborn leaves sing alone just like me   stuck
here in the middle of everywhere

The Lonely Road

ROBYN BISHOP

Time is slow in the garden. A slight breeze blows through the gums and the ferns, and rustles Annie's grey hair as she lounges on a bench and reads. The dogs lie at her feet with their heads on their paws. She loops her fingers through Jesse the border collie's wiry white coat and sighs with contentment. A truck horn blasts on the other side of her fence and she jumps, holding her breath until she hears the vehicle's door slam shut and heavy footsteps crunching away from her on next door's gravel.

Laying down her book she rises, her gypsy skirt falling smoothly to her ankles. The dogs follow her across the buffalo grass and pant as she picks orange lilies, red roses and purple agapanthus to decorate her studio. Inside, Jesse's wagging tail knocks over a jar of water and Annie's paintbrushes clatter onto the floor. She rubs her arthritic back as she bends to retrieve them and place them on the easel's lip. A girl riding a bike smiles at her from the canvas. It's one in a series of female portraits that Annie is working on. The girl doesn't wear a helmet. She's from the 1970s and is free to ride without encumberment. She is Annie before the rape.

Robbo laughed as Nic dragged Annie from the back seat of the orange Datsun and shoved her onto the grass. She looked for help but the dark carpark was empty except for a mongrel dog sniffing at an overflowing rubbish bin under a street lamp.

"What do you think you're doing?" asked Annie, trying to still the panic in her voice.

"Play nice," growled Nic, "and you'll be all right."

"I want to go to Molly's place … you said you'd take me," she said.

"And we will. After you do something for us.'

"I thought we were friends."

Nic laughed. "Oh, we are baby, we are. We'll be best friends soon."

"I want to go now, please." Annie tried to run.

Nic grabbed her arm and threatened, "I've got a knife."

She felt it, hard in the small of her back and went limp.

"That's better. Down there on the beach. Go." He pushed her down a sharp incline and she stumbled, face planting in the sand. "Pull her pants down Robbo, right down."

"No," said Annie. "Don't. I'll scream."

Nic dug the knife in her back. Even through her parka she could feel the blade. He pulled her beanie off, threw it across the sand and twisted his fingers through her dark curls.

She whimpered.

Robbo struggled with her jeans. "Undo them," he barked.

She fumbled with the buckle. It bit into her fingers. He twisted her onto her back, unzipped her fly, flipped her over again and tugged awkwardly at her jeans until her bottom was bare in the chilly air.

"On your knees, bitch."

When she resisted, he shoved her face in the sand and yanked her up. She couldn't breathe.

"What an arse you've got Annie, what a beautiful arse." Nic smacked her hard. It stung. "Me first mate, then you."

Robbo grunted.

Nic roughly parted her legs, mounted her and thrust into her. She screamed as brutal raw pain ripped her apart. He took no notice and rode her, grunting and groaning like a wild beast. She dug her fingernails into the sand and sobbed until he shot his hot sticky load into her, shuddered and rolled off. She tried to crawl away but Robbo, stinking of beer and strong sweat, caught her.

"No you don't. It's my turn."

She didn't struggle. This time it didn't hurt as much. She lay still and prayed it would soon be over. The surf roared onto the beach. Strange how she hadn't noticed it until now. She shouldn't have hitchhiked. Her mum had told her it wasn't safe. But how else was she going to get to Molly's eighteenth birthday when she'd missed the last bus from Frankston to Sorrento? And the men had seemed nice at first, playing cassettes she liked in the Datsun and offering her smokes and stubbies. She didn't like beer but she'd drunk it anyway, not wanting to be impolite. They'd laughed and told jokes and teased her about her frizzy hair and her rainbow coloured home knitted beanie. She'd liked them and thought they liked her. Don't be so naïve Annie, she could hear her mother say. If only her mother was here now.

Robbo finished, rolled off her and lay next to her panting. "Nice, Annie, nice," he moaned.

She turned over numbly and stared at the sky, wondering when the stars had come out. She heaved up her jeans, ignoring the repellent wetness and the ache between her legs, wiped sand and snot from her nose and struggled to her feet. She began to walk up the beach, craving a hot shower. Nic followed her while Robbo pissed on the sand.

Nic seized her arm. "I didn't realise you were a virgin. You came on to us pretty strongly in the car. Like you were asking for it."

She shrugged him off.

"Come on. It wasn't that bad was it?"

"You said you'd take me to Molly's," she whispered.

"Yeah and we will. But if you tell anyone about this we'll find you and …"

"And what?"

"Something really bad will happen to you."

She stared at him.

"You better believe it bitch," he growled before turning to the beach and calling out, "Get a move on Robbo, haven't got all night."

Annie sat on the bench outside the courtroom and fiddled with the skirt of the knee-length brown dress she'd borrowed from her mother to make her appear innocent and respectable. Normally, she wore bright colours, outrageous patterned tights and short skirts and shopped in op shops, unable to afford anything more expensive while she studied art at university. The money she earned waitressing barely covered the rent of her share house in Brunswick.

Even though it'd been ten months since she was raped she often woke screaming in the night as if Nic and Robbo were pushing her down on her bed, ramming into her and suffocating her. In the daytime she tried to bury them in a corner of her brain. But they surfaced when she least expected them to and she felt dizzy and nauseous until she stumbled into a room and locked the door. Small, locked rooms and bright lights were the only thing that made her feel safe.

As the trial dragged into the fourth week she wished she hadn't been talked into reporting the rape to the police by Molly's well-meaning mum, Edith. Edith had sent everyone home from the eighteenth birthday party, shooed Molly to bed, bundled Annie into the car and drove her to the police station, saying, "It's the right thing to do Annie. You'll thank me later. Besides, you can't just let them go free, think how you'd feel if they violated some other poor girl."

They'd waited a long time to be seen and when the detective on duty dissected her story, Annie had felt like a helpless bug under a microscope. She'd excused herself to go to the bathroom and thought about crawling out the window the way she'd seen a prisoner do in *Division 4* but Edith knocked on the door and returned her to the detective, who was deep in conversation with a constable. A sob had caught in Annie's throat. The constable held her rainbow coloured beanie.

"Found it on the back beach, Sir. Exactly where the girl said it would be. Reckon this one is telling the truth."

"Can I have a shower now?" Annie had whispered. "And I'd like my beanie back."

"No love, physical examination first, then a shower," the detective had said, "and the beanie is evidence. Sorry I was harsh with my line of questioning, but you never know when someone is lying."

Edith had snapped, "Why on earth would a girl lie about something like this Detective Thomas?"

"Ahh, when you've seen the things I've seen …" He'd shrugged. "By the way, the name's Doug." He'd looked at Annie with compassion for the first time. "Can you call me Doug, Annie? We'll be seeing a bit of each other now I'm taking on the case."

Annie had nodded. She wanted to sleep and never wake up.

Doug had led her into an examination room with a hospital bed and a doctor. The doctor had talked calmly while Edith helped her undress. Annie had no idea what he was saying as he handed her a backless gown, helped her onto the bed and pried her legs apart. She was numb, a lump of flesh, nothing more. She'd been vaguely aware of a spatula inside her, swabs being taken and her clothes being placed in a plastic bag before her mother burst into the room and gathered her in her arms.

Her mother had encouraged her to swallow the morning after pill, helped her to the shower and turned on the hot water. Annie had huddled on the floor, unable to wash herself, wishing only to disappear down the drain.

The courtroom door swung open. Annie checked her watch. It was 9 a.m. precisely. She chewed her cheek and walked in with her mother and Edith by her side. Doug followed them, patting her briefly on the back. Her lawyer, who had been provided by the state, swept past in his gown and nodded. He'd shocked her a couple of days ago by saying, "You know Annie, this is not worth it. If it ever happens to you again just lie back and enjoy it as much as you can then forget about it."

She sat down and looked at the floor as the jurors, mostly middle-aged men, filed in. When she'd told them the intimate details of the rape on the witness stand last week, their faces had been impassive. She'd felt as if she were the one on trial, not Nic and Robbo.

They rose as the judge entered, his wig slightly lopsided, his face grim. Today the jury would deliver their verdict.

Annie surveys her paintings that line the studio walls and are spread across the floor. She's preparing for an exhibition in the Wonthaggi Town Hall next week. When she told her secondary school students about it, they had gathered around her in an excited mass.

"Oh Miss, you're going to be famous!"

"Can we come?"

"What do you paint Miss? You've never told us."

"I paint women," replied Annie, smiling.

She didn't tell them that the women represented various phases in her own life: her innocence before the rape; the days she couldn't get out of bed after Nic and Robbo walked free; her graduation when she got so drunk she passed out; the various locked rooms of her life where she kept the light on all night and the days where she'd witnessed girlfriends get married and pretended to be happy.

She sighs and runs her fingers across the layered paint of the self-portrait she began after she finally went to counselling. Violent reds and oranges surround her; her face is grey and filled with pain. She hadn't talked about the rape since the trial 30 years ago; she'd kept it inside. The release afterwards was enormous. She cried for days and surfaced less ashamed and calmer.

Surrounding the self-portrait are miniatures of the older women in her painting group, Women, who proudly wear their mileage on their faces and have their own stories to tell. Women who have survived. This is how Annie sees herself now, as a survivor. She jumps at loud noises and keeps a night light burning but she is still here and as whole as she can possibly be.

The centrepiece for the exhibition rests on the mantle above her fireplace. It's of her female students, ready to confront the world, and shines with hope.

It's All Connected

DIANE BELL

"Downstream whingers." Bluey Blanks, of ruddy complexion at the best of times, was fire-engine red. He had just endured a 'Let's talk about water' workshop at the Mechanics Hall in the otherwise quiet hamlet of Milang on the banks of Lake Alexandrina in South Australia.

"Sure, it's the driest state in the driest continent and a long time since the last rains, but let's get some perspective here—some bloody inedible endangered fish needs water to spawn? Some smelly lake needs to flush? Damn these doomsday bludgers. What about the real work, up here in the food bowl? It's our jobs, our property, our rights, our water."

He strode across to his Toyota Land Cruiser, threw a sheaf of glossy 'Drought Resilience' brochures onto the back seat, and headed back to the airport. He had important business in his electorate in Queensland and needed to make the last flight out of Adelaide. City of Churches be buggered.

"Upstream bastards," Dave Keller muttered, as he farewelled the Minister for Environment, Development and Community and ambled inside to rejoin the unlikely alliance of dairy farmers, grape-growers, fisher-people, conservationists, scientists, and traditional owners who had gathered to hear what the Minister had to offer. They were already exchanging mobile numbers and email contacts. The local IT expert, sorely tried by the lack of reliable broadband, offered to create a spreadsheet. "We could try a website," he suggested.

"Hard copy for me," Dave laughed. "Now, let's talk about the *River*."

The community urn was on the boil. Joyce's legendary scones were being buttered and spread with local jam and cream. Rural folk knew how to socialise and strategise. Within an hour they had a plan, a real plan, with timelines, teams, and tasks. Dave loaded the dishwasher, locked up and drove home to Joyce who was finishing up in the milking shed. Dave beamed and gave her a thumbs up. "Scone diplomacy, my love. Worked a treat."

Joyce held the screen door for Dave. "We have a visitor."

"Ha. Dee Scrutari, my favourite niece. Loved your posts on the Nile River crisis, but do I have a story for you!" He spread out the large canvas he was carrying and they pored over the hand-drawn map of the Murray-Darling Basin, read the coloured post-it notes: names, addresses, key words, urls, dates, and questions. "This is *our* MDB Plan. Our stories. Our conflicts. Our strategies. Want in? We could do with some of that anthropological nouse of yours."

Dee had been following the story of the so-called 'Millennium Drought' from Uganda. It was international news. 'Blue Gold' was what Maude Barlow, senior advisor to the President of the UN General Assembly, called the dwindling global supply of potable water, a trigger for World War Three. Dee was desperate to get into the field, walk the country with the traditional owners, listen to their stories, meet with local interest groups, interrogate the competing narratives of the key players. Would the stories of the pioneering heroes of original owners of what was now called the 'Murray-Darling Basin' resonate with the epic struggle being played out in the 21st century 'Water Wars'? Was Maude's community-based campaigning to have water declared a human right the big-picture framing that could cut across the internecine conflict that Dave and Joyce were now outlining?

When the fault lines of a culture opened wide, when the core values of a society were starkly drawn, Dee was in her element. In a brand new notebook, she wrote:

Primary tenet of ecology and a foundational belief of Aboriginal culture: 'It's all connected'. How to map the macro-narratives of the ecologists, economists, and engineers with the micro-narratives of the river communities?

Soaring salinity levels threatened dairy farmers like the Kellers. They'd raised prime cattle on the banks of the lakes for generations.

"Diversify? Low interest loans? We're already deep in debt from buying water to keep our stock alive." Book-keeper Joyce was having none of that advice.

Dave jabbed at the map. "See all the family farms that have folded."

Joyce, who followed the market and read the *Stock Journal*, identified the root cause. "Multi-national agri-businesses are sucking the life out the river system to make profit for shareholders. How much rice and cotton can we eat?"

Dave nodded. "Our produce is the pride of the nation. Iced coffee anyone? It's Farmer's Union."

Dee was studying the map. "Tell me about these tags on your plan." Green post-it note: 'Let the River flow'. Red: 'Over-allocation'. Orange: 'Economic doom'. Brown: 'Dams, weirs, pipelines'.

"The Murray Mouth is silted over. Dredges working 24/7. There's two million tonnes of upstream salt to be flushed though the Mouth to the Southern Ocean every year. We're trying to find common ground," Dave explained. "But each interest group has its own expert and the modelling is being weaponised by the pollies. And secrets. Commercial-in-confidence, that kinda crap."

"And climate change?" Dee asked.

"Bluey Blanks is promoting Lord Monckton." Dave regaled Dee with the so-called 'debates', on talk-back radio.

Dee wrote:

Contradictions, contestings and conflicts: When did science become dueling opinions? By what logic is one climate denier to be given equal time with 100 climate scientists? When did Cartesian skepticism become conspiracy theory?

Dee was inspecting the name and occupation tags on the map. "How the hell did you get all these folk to the meeting?"

"Networking."

"Show me." As Joyce and Dave skipped from tag to tag, they were tracking marriages, school histories, and sporting affiliations. They laid out photograph albums, local histories, and newspaper clippings; told stories of bores sunk deep into the limestone and plans for desalination plants.

"But what we want and what the River *needs* is a long-term plan, based on the best science. That's the sum of these tags. What do you reckon Dee?"

"Let's sleep on it."

"Bunk down in the back room. You'll get a signal there. I know you're itching to get online."

"Thanks Dave. Can we go to the Mouth tomorrow?"

"Easy as."

Dee wrote:

The stories are powerful, passionate and political but they're told in different languages. Water is a commodity: The River is a living body.

Dee logged on and began searching, correlating chronologies with genealogies. She was looking for connections. It wasn't long before she had identified key families whose interests in the River reached back beyond the proclamation of the State of South Australia in 1836. One strand piqued her interest: the 19th century phenomenon of theatre in pubs, cheap and accessible, but killed off by 6 o'clock closing in the early 20th century. Did that singing tradition persist? In the Kellers' old photograph albums, Dee found memorabilia of community performances and tagged them for future investigation.

> *Was music a common denominator? If they couldn't talk about the River, could they sing about it? A plaintive solo? Conciliatory duet? Rousing chorus?*

Dee fell asleep and dreamed in rhyming couplets: scientist/iron fist; engineer/Belgian beer.

Morning milking completed, they headed off across the barrages built in the 1930s to hold back the sea, and onto the Mouth. The dredges churned. The pumps throbbed. It was visceral. A River on end-of-life support.

> *Oh, that the Murray Mouth could speak. Shipwrecks, tragic drownings, heroic rescues, the traditional owners' commitment to protecting their sites, including women's sites on Hindmarsh Island, where fresh and saltwater meet, where ngatji (totems) proliferate, Kumarangk (place of birth).*

Dee was singing to herself as she walked through the pipis to the *ngori* (pelicans) massing on the exposed sandbar. "I've got a list …"

Joyce joined in. "Of society offenders who might well be underground …"

"And don't I know them?" Dave enumerated a cast of characters he would cheerfully consign to history. "Quite a tradition at family gatherings to parody Gilbert and Sullivan. *The Mikado* was a favourite."

"That's how we met," Joyce volunteered. "Musical theatre ran in our family. Did you know Granddad sang in the pubs before World War One?"

"What about Gilbert and Sullivan?" Dee asked.

"Well, that was later, like 1930s onwards," Dave said. "Jack Higgs, founding member of the G & S Society. I knew him. Well, we all did." He was on a roll: more names, places, songs.

This is the cut-through, feuding families, united by deep time origin stories, brought to resolution in a grand finale. The generative power of the meeting of the waters.

"Fancy calling into Camp Coorong?" Dee asked.

"Maybe visit the Meningie bakery on the way through?" Joyce suggested. "I told Auntie Evie I'd be there some time later today. I know she'd love to see you. She often talks about how good you were when her mum passed away."

"Well, that connection goes way back."

"Like to the early days of the Protector's camp at Wellington on the Murray?"

"Hum, you know?" Dee nodded. "I kinda guessed when I was doing the family lines last night."

"Well, dear Dee, write a note about this then. Those Old People loved to sing, *Pakari Nganawi Ruwi,* 'Prayer for country', and hymns, carols, love songs, show tunes. They were in demand, beautiful harmonies."

Aunty Evie was weaving, a master class for post-graduates from Adelaide Uni. "Join us. We were just yarning about how the rushes need fresh water. Salinity makes them brittle. That's our science, from our Old People."

Over lunch, Aunty Evie updated them about progress on the 'Letters Patent' of 1836, a foundational document with the potential to rewrite the history of land tenure in South Australia. Her uncles had already brought news about the Milang meeting.

Bush telegraph, more reliable than Telstra. Dee showed Aunty Evie the genealogies she'd drawn. Dave and Joyce scrolled through their mobiles for photos of concerts past.

"It's all connected," Aunty Evie said as she finished the sister basket she was weaving for an exhibition with PoMo weavers in California. "The stories, the families, the country, the River."

"Can we sing it?" Dee asked.

"How about *The Pirates of Penzance*? Bring Bluey to the table?" Dave, a natural baritone, began

I am the very model of a Murray Darling manager,
I've information scientific, cul'tral, and economical
I know the names of rorters, and can cite reports historical
From Water Acts to IGAs in order categorical;
I'm very well acquainted too, with matters ecological,
I understand salinity from seven to astronomical,
About low flow modelling I'm teeming with a lot o' news,
With many cheerful facts about the pollies who are best to schmooze.

"And add this for the irrigators, apologies to Koko," Joyce added:

As one day it will happen that a victim must be found
I've got a little list—I've got a little list
Of water rorters who might well be underground
And who never would be missed—who never would be missed!

Dave couldn't resist. "Don't forget the 'merchant bankers'. Thanks Opera Australia."

Aunty Evie was humming along. "Nanna knew those tunes."

"Can we join in?" The science grad-students had been listening. "Here's one for ecological modelers."

Three little gals from school are we,
Smart with our numbers you will see,
Shocked to the bone with hyperbole,
Three nimble gals from school.

"And a storyline? One that recognises conflict but finds connection?"

"*Ringballin* [ceremony]. We danced the River from the Mouth to the source, brought everyone together, all the nations up the River."

"Dave, reckon, your IT expert can rally the troops for a community meeting?" Dee asked.

"Resilience? You ain't seen nothing yet."

An unexpected storm blew in from Kangaroo Island. The Elders said it was a sign. The barrages were briefly opened, flows restored. The mood improved. The show gained momentum, from one Mechanics Hall to the next. The *River* was celebrated. Future use projections were grounded in the deep history of connections and local knowledge. 'Climate change' became a character and sang of 'Lying awake with a dreadful headache'. 'Salinity' was unmasked as the evil twin of 'greed'. Upstream/ downstream family-based dialogues developed. Bluey lost his seat. The PoMo weavers sent a basket of hope. By acknowledging the 'Letters Patent', South Australia was restored as a human rights haven. Maude Barlow wrote an epilogue celebrating the new egalitarian social order: "When everyone is somebodee, then no one's anybody!"

Did it really happen like that? #FictionConnects.

Christmas Hills Rhapsody

SANDY JEFFS

And so I dare to hope
Though changed, no doubt, from what I
was when first
I came among these hills …

Wordsworth, Tintern Abbey

1

As my small silver Hyundai, engine humming,
wheels turning in mechanical synchronicity,
glides over Kangaroo Ground hill—
to the left of me the old memorial tower
surrounded by sprawling plump vineyards
and the Summer-yellow paddocks
dry with the season's water lack
and rustling grasses quivering in the heat
where kangaroo mobs once peacefully grazed
before a culling disappeared them—
I am welcomed to this ancient Wurundjeri country
once strode by its custodians.

2

Crossing this hill, I escape the harried world
of monotonous suburbs, manic freeways,
high-rise monsters, infested air,

people cheek by jowl,
and I am heading northwards,
just a few country-kilometres
along the Eltham-Yarra Glen Road,
past Henley Road, gateway to the Bend of Islands,
and onto the much-loved Kangaroo Ground Cemetery
where the dead lie peacefully in rural tranquillity,
then coasting through shady Watsons Creek
with its popular Dark Horse Café
and over a bridge that spans a small stream
before winding my way through
the sharp, accident-prone bends.
And rounding more sweeping curves
through uneven, craggy terrain,
suddenly, on my left, is Clintons Road
which takes you to neighbouring Smiths Gully,
and immediately on my right is
the Simpson Road turn-off which runs
to the cursed dam
whose rising waters not so long ago
split our area and identity in half.
Further on is sleepy Happy Valley
where, in earlier times, gold fever lured fossickers
and then, sitting in amongst the trees
is a surprise rustic primary school.
Not far from there, closer to home now,
is the Montsalvat farm
while across the road sits the old, derelict post office.
And if this road is taken afar,

it leads you down a steep hill and into the
Yarra Valley and the hamlet of Yarra Glen
where greenie and redneck politics collide.

3

I am bound for my Christmas Hills anchorage
where scrubby eucalypts with chaotic canopies
like grand monarchs stand tall
and gullies of tussock grass
tumble downwards to dams,
and orchids are sprinkled like fairy dust
on the leaf-littered ground.
I feel so blessed that, after a long odyssey,
through the city's asphalt streets,
dark places of menacing man-made design,
I can return to my quiet wonderland.
And this homeward journey
is necessary to salve my threadbare soul
made ragged by the assault of urban warlords.
This humble place amongst the gums
is my shelter and sanity.

4

The ageless land on which we trespass
and from whose core we have strayed
nevertheless, is my home
where I have walked and slumbered,
cackled and cried for over forty years—
a blip in First Nations' time—
but for my few stolen years
it seems ever so long.

5

What to make of the clock's ceaseless ticking
and time passing and
friends ageing towards decline?
And cats and dogs having come and gone
from our animalia home,

a grim marker of ephemeral time.
What to make of my own body's
regression to a weaker physical state
where I am no longer the young whippet,
though I remain so in my mind's eye?
Time teases me with its tedious days
but O how the months and years fly by
and age crawls upon me like a snake
curling its mouth around a helpless mouse.
As the seasons roll on, relentless,
and when Winter becomes fire-worrying Summer,
I battle the mental fear of disaster.
And yet I cannot stop the clock,
or the seasons or the descent into age.
I am wearied by the rhythm of life
and Fate's humourless jokes.

6
And yet, these hills console me
wrapping me in a sylvan rug
where I am snug against the railing storms
where time is tamed briefly
and I can loaf and loiter without care.
Just knowing I am in the midst
of this ancient land,
not having to step out amongst it
but to watch it from my window
gives me comfort.
And to see the rainbow lorikeets and
king parrots bluster around,
to hear the magpies warble
and the jester-laughing kookaburras,
all a symphonic chorus,

soothes my troubles.
I am forever moved to great emotion,
bigger and stronger than I am able to give to words.

7
I look to other poets for inspiration,
poets who have walked leafy laneways
and rambled over brooks,
their words always a measure above my feeble poems.
How they have shown us the way
with pens that conjure their solitude and joy.
I write in their shadow—
perhaps too full of my own poetic self
yet knowing I am a poet of no distinction.
But for each word I put upon this page
a tear falls from each and every letter
to mark the grief that besets us all in this world,
a world too modern for a crone like me.

8
But I return to my eternal home
my shelter from the world's wars,
the looming climate catastrophe,
the Market's pull on our lives,
the techno cacophony,
the social media eruptions,
democracy in retreat,
autocrats rising across the world
like paranoid Putin deluded that
he can make Russia great again,
the resurfacing of antisemitism,
and American women suddenly finding
they are living in Gilead,
while my rainbow brethren and mad comrades

fight crippling stigma.
Then there are the corrupt and shameless
politicians who beg, woo, flatter and lie
for our precious vote.
And yes, they have stirred the fuming cynic in me.
I have rage roiling in my blood,
so much is wrong in our film noir lives.

9
Yet, this place where it is
Christmas every day, calms my rage
and soothes the clangour in my heart.
I listen for the birdsong
and for the rustle of lizards on the ground
while our restful vegie garden mellows
and the chooks scurry about in their pen.
And in my study,
feeling secure amongst the hanging Balinese angels,
the books that line the walls,
Russian and Greek Orthodox icons
and religious trinketry, full of irony,
watch over an atheistic me,
and my desk that is piled high with papers and tomes,
I find much needed consolation.
I am centred and safe
and brave enough to pour my heart into a mystery
never knowing if a shade
will fall between my first draft and final copy.

10
My words will never be like
the ancient stories that join
tribes to ancestors long gone.
My words are contemporary,

meagre attempts to find a common chord,
a scale of moving syllables reaching their zenith
in my latter-day hymn.
But great poets have known things
long before science or psychology or
academics examined the mind.
They have sensed with their hearts
and written with their imaginations
delving deep into the secrets
that drive our primal instincts.
And they have found a timeless language.

11
And it is instinct that
joins me with the trees and shrubs
and wind and rain, the sun, moon and stars,
the raw impulses that nature
calls us to share with her
as she holds us in her repertoire of moving moods.
My home in the hills is my queendom,
my domain, my country,
my realm of natural gifts.
It guards my heart from
a deep, sad current that would
sometimes well like a floodtide
and I, powerless to resist it,
would sink beneath its melancholy weight.
And worse, madness lurks deep
in my mind's crevices.

12
What will it be like when I can no longer
dance with the evening dusk
or dawdle in the morning dawn?

When I am far away from my beloved hills
stuck in some aged care home,
sentient or not—
who knows what the future holds?
My mind may give way and
travel far from reality's realm
locked up in a demented purgatory,
flailing for thought,
trying to place my friends,
when time is neither here nor there,
forgetting who I am.
Will my heart remember my hills
and the joy they gave me?
Or will my hills sink like ancient Atlantis
and remain submerged
until an explorer, brave of heart,
raises my memory to the surface?
Who knows?
But when my last breath is drawn,
after many years wandering across these slopes
and through my mind's mystical valleys,
will upon my lips feather the words 'my hills',
and will I bask in my handsome home
upon a homecoming reckoning?
Or will my solitary walk upon a pathway
sprinkled with the sleeping dust of Morpheus
light my way to forgetfulness?
No! The bucolic idyll that held my core as one
cannot be broken.
It is where we find ourselves when
everywhere and everything and everyone
is lost in the temporal temple with its
prowling bitumen serpents and concrete canker

and the barren glass and steel and bricks and mortar dwellings.
My Arcadian hills, *our* Christmas Hills,
are for me dear and true
where we live in our cherished pastoral dream.

Kalifornia, her color

USHA AKELLA

The fires began in a heaven splintering in the dark,
a multi-veined pyrotechnic-sky running white light
striking the candlestick-trees with
fire impersonating itself instantaneously
into a many-tongued goddess dancing wildly,
windstorms aided the torrid air simmering in coral hue,
a great deluge of light consuming manmade light
licking the land, a crematory blaze of funeral pyres,
then dry and cindered.

In the eerie auburn glow
the burnished redwoods—
a lineage of glory, in the hazy coral-apricot
melted-sun-air—tremble as feathers,
burning tandoors their wombs aflame.
Heaped houses and power outaged acres,
asthmatic ash-aired counties spasming
in submission to a tangerine fury,
to a tiger-orange animal in heat unrestrained
leaving charcoal dark footprints,
in this country where they formulate a woman at size zero
here, she dances in voluptuous
saffron-sindoor-amber-apricot-
apfelsine-salmon splendor.

The Child-thief

BULBUL SHARMA

They taught me to steal when I was six years old.

"She is the right size now," said my father one morning, staring at me like a butcher, assessing whether the goat he was about to slaughter was the right weight or not. My mother nodded without looking up.

It was a moonless night as my father and I walked through the silent streets of a rich neighbourhood, far away from the slums where we lived. The gardens had brightly painted children's swings and big blue tubs filled with water with yellow, plastic ducks floating in them. Some gardens even had little houses for their dogs and I was imagining what kind of food these dogs ate when I was startled by my father jabbing me in the arm. The street lamps cast a yellow light on his face, changing his features and making him suddenly look like a stranger to me. He pointed to a house a little ahead of us. We started walking faster now. The street lamp was not lit outside the house. The high iron gate was shut but the wall that encircled the house had a narrow crack which was easy for us to scale. We jumped into the garden, falling on the dew-drenched grass on silent, naked feet. We stood frozen for a few seconds. I had been trained to stand still without breathing from the time I was two years old. My mother had made me balance on the edge of the wall outside our shed and slapped me hard if I fell. I learnt very quickly to stay absolutely still. You just had to hold your breath.

The grass felt soft under my bare feet. No dogs barked. No guard shouted. My father had done his homework well. There was a large balcony covered with flowering creepers and below it a tiny barred window.

"Go. Go in quietly and then open the door for me," whispered my father as he gently pushed me through the window. I was a thin child with long arms. I was the perfect shape for a thief, my mother often said when she bathed me. I slipped in through the bars, wriggling like an eel and when my bare feet touched the cold floor, I waited. "Wait till your eyes can see in the dark," my father had said to me. Everyone at home had been very excited about my first outing as a thief. My mother had plaited my hair and tied on a new ribbon. She made jaggery sweets and fed me with her hands.

The room was silent and totally dark but the tables and chairs seem to glisten with a hidden light. There were silver ornaments everywhere, winking at me. I held my breath and then when my eyes could see properly, I stepped forward. The door was on the far end of the room and it seemed to get further away as I walked towards it. My heart was hitting my chest so hard that I felt it would burst out of my body. My knees began trembling and I fell on the floor. I began to crawl on my hands and feet. I crawled slowly but my heart was racing as if I was running. "You are a snake, creeping in the grass. No one can see you or hear you," I said to myself. My breathing calmed. The bolt on the door slid down almost on its own and in a flash of a second, my father was in the room. I had done my task.

Soon, I was the best thief in my family. I had to be, otherwise we would starve. My father now lay in bed, drunk all the time. My mother had had a miscarriage and died. The baby had died too. Just as well, since there was hardly any food in the house now.

We were hungry all the time and often had to scavenge around for scraps on the streets. My father only wanted a bottle of hooch that was brewed by one of the women in our slum colony. I did chores for her and she gave me a bottle every two or three days that kept my father happy.

When my brother Shyam turned 14, life became easier. He joined a gang that worked in the parking lot, stealing mobile phones and any other stuff people left in their cars. Soon he was almost as good at thieving as I was.

"You will be surprised to see how many expensive things people leave in their cars. Sometimes we don't even have to break open the car window. They leave it open for us. It is as if they want us to take all these things away from them so that they can buy more," he laughed.

"Can I come with you one day?" I asked. Those days I was doing the rounds of the crowded markets, stealing bags, phones and any thing else my nimble fingers could pick up. I later sold them to a man who specialized in handling stolen goods. I took care not to work in the same markets more than once or twice in case someone recognized me. I am a very pretty girl.

"Not a good thing for a thief to have a beautiful face," grumbled my brother, so I often put black spots on my face to look ugly. So far I had never been caught.

But now I wanted to steal something really big that would feed us for a few months and then I could rest for a while. When I saw young girls of my age roaming around with friends, chatting and laughing, I felt so jealous. I brushed past them and swiped something from their bags. These silly little things never fetched any money but it made me feel better.

"You can come with us tomorrow, Pinky. I have cleared it with Boss-bhai," said my brother.

The Boss-bhai was a lame man who lived next door to us. When I was a child he had pinched my cheeks with his twisted fingers and left a bruise. He always stared at me when I walked past and I could feel his half-closed eyes piercing my skin like needles.

"You must stay very quiet if the cops appear. Remember, they will not do anything to us since Boss-bhai pays them regularly every week," said Shyam.

"Have you ever seen me cry, you idiot?' I said and gave him a gentle slap on his head.

It was late evening when we walked into the underground parking lot of the new shopping mall not far from our slums. A well-dressed young couple came out of the lift, loaded with shopping bags, talking in excited voices. "I got those Nike shoes for only five thousand. Did you see the new Apple watch? Too expensive. I am glad I got the Fitbit instead."

"I found a lovely new lipstick shade. Look. Honey rust," said the girl.

I could smell the scent on the girl's skin. Her hands looked so soft and each of her fingernails was painted a different colour. I wondered if anyone had ever hit her. They did not notice us. We were dressed in our best clothes—our working clothes—and looked almost as smart as them. Boss-bhai was sitting in his van in the parking lot. Though he was far away, I could feel his eyes watching me.

We followed the shoppers right to their car. My brother suddenly pretended to trip and fell against the boy. As the boy turned around to help him, I picked the wallet from his pocket and took his new Fitbit. They waved to us as they drove away. Fools.

Then we saw another couple walking past. Our prey. We were going to try a new trick. It needed two people to make it work.

We began to follow them. They were arguing with each other loudly and the woman kept swinging her handbag in an agitated way.

"Perfect. Fight on, my lovelies," said my brother. We waited until the couple reached their car and got in, still arguing. As the man started up the car, the woman threw all her shopping bags into the back seat. Then she threw her handbag too. Nice.

I moved forward.

"Sir … Madam, excuse me, I think you have dropped something," I said in my polite, smooth voice. I had learnt to speak like this from watching TV.

The man, startled, stared at me. I pointed to the floor. Five one hundred rupee notes were scattered on the dirty, cement floor.

"Oh! No! You stupid woman! Look!" yelled the man as he got out of the car. The woman hesitated. We held our breath. Come on, I willed her. Then she came out too.

"What are you shouting about?" she said, waving her hands about.

The man, his wife and I all looked at the notes lying on the ground. "You must have dropped this from your bag, Madam," I said.

"You are so careless," said her husband.

"How are you so sure that I dropped the money?" she retorted. "It could have fallen from your back pocket. You are forever scratching your bum," she muttered.

I bent down and picked up the notes. They were wet and muddy. Our hard-earned money. But we had had to use the notes as bait.

The woman moved back but the man took the notes from me. Then they got into the car and drove away, arguing loudly. Shyam and I ran to the van. Boss-bhai took the shopping bags, the handbag and all the other stuff Shyam had lifted from the back seat of the car. We drove away.

Shyam and I sauntered back to the mall for a well-earned ice-cream. Boss-bhai would give us our cut later on. He was a great miser and we had to often beg him for the money that was rightfully ours. We had earned it while he just sat in the van, whistling and staring at me.

That is when I got the idea. "Why not do this on our own? We do all the work. Why should he get a share?" I asked.

"He knows how to get rid of the stolen stuff."

"We can do it too."

"Pinky, I don't want to take the risk."

"We do take the risk. He just sits in the car."

We went to the mall again the next day. I played the same trick on an elderly couple. They took so long to understand what I was saying that I almost gave up but finally the old man came out of the car to pick up the notes I had scattered on the parking lot floor.

"Maybe they belong to someone else. We should check with the security guard," he said and my heart sank. An honest person really makes it difficult for us to play this trick. We need greed to make it work. I waited.

"You must have dropped them," said his wife, looking sadly at the old man.

While I talked to the old couple, my brother slipped into the car and took out the shopping bags. He only had a few minutes but he was fast. He ran with the stuff to the van, threw it in and then we walked away quickly. Boss-bhai was starting the van when the cops arrived. He ignored them. But these were not Boss-bhai's pet cops that he had bribed. These were new women cops I had called on my phone. They took Boss-bhai away in handcuffs. At last, I was free of his hateful eyes.

I am the boss now. I will steal hard. When I have enough money, my brother and I will stop. We will become ordinary people.

One day we will forget we were thieves once.

The Thief Danced On

GENA COREA

The drums drew Francisca Melaco up, pulled her body, ample in its fifty-five years, skin ebony against the white of her lacy blouse and the blue of her bandanna, pulled her up to her feet, eyes closed, face tilted to the sky. A photographer snapped her, arms outstretched, shoulders shimmying. Majestic.

String and wind instruments throbbed atop the Trio Electrico, a huge truck fitted with a bandstand so high, it nearly reached the palms swaying on the coconut trees in the gentle February night breeze.

It was carnival in Salvador da Bahia in Brazil and Francisca was here to jump it with the thousands of other Bahians sambaing through the streets. She wore the blue and white of her orisha, Yemanjá mother of the waters, goddess of the waves.

Scores of Trio Electricos slowly sailed through the streets, like giant ships of music. Each was accompanied by a 'bloco', several hundred people who had hired the Trio and danced to its music in a moveable space around it, delineated by thick ropes. Young men hired to maintain that space against crowds surging towards the music, wore thick gloves and held the ropes taut.

On the sidewalk, a hill of husks grew high as a vendor pushed sugarcane through a crusher and caught, in a waiting cup, the sweet casha that gushed forth. Beside him, thick red slabs of watermelon dripped with juice on a board over a stack of crates.

At the feet of the vendor, piles of green watermelons waited to be sliced into red.

Two bare-chested men carried crates of beer over their heads, dancing through the crowd to the beat of the samba. The man behind them balanced an ice block that dripped on his muscled shoulder, leaving a wedge of wet on his shirt.

Suddenly, a wiry woman leapt into the space beside Francisca, faced her and danced fiercely, with a power that called forth Francisca's own. They played together. When the music stopped, they threw themselves into each other's arms in shrieks of joy, kissing cheeks, holding each other's chins with tenderness. Francisca unwrapped the bandana from her head and wiped sweat from the fierce dancer's face. Then they parted, these two women who had never before met but had now connected from a place deeper than words.

Above Francisca, people hung out of windows in the upper stories of houses along the road, stood on roofs, on tiny balconies of wrought iron, on window ledges, grinning, waving, singing. Excited children and youths stood in trees strung with lights, watching the dancers below them—half-nude bodies writhing in the air charged by pounding drums. Some danced recklessly on the bobbing branches.

Carn-eval: Giving permission to the body.

Francisca loved the physicality of carnival; her body dripping with her own sweat and that of the people pressing against her. The sensual swaying and circling of hips as singers belted their lyrics: "I have God in my heart and the devil in my pelvis." Cold beer running down her throat. The pressure of a slowly filling bladder—

Francisca had to pee.

She sambaed down a steep hill heading for a dark cul-de-sac. She could have stayed right there under the lights like one of her white friends who she'd seen an hour earlier squatting by the street curb, one hand holding her panties to the side, a blissful expression on her face as her water gushed into the gutter. Francisca had laughed, watching her friend, who was the Director of Nurses in the University's School of Public Health. Laughed, loving Bahia and these bodies that danced and pissed.

When she reached the dark street down the hill, the stench was overwhelming. She squatted, peed, stood, and caught the eye of another woman, sinewy, with a blue ribbon round her head, just rising from the same task. They grinned and swayed back up the hill in silence, lifting their full skirts to shelter their noses.

Francisca broke the silence, intoning, as if reading a sacred text: "And Jesus Christ asked her for the third time: 'Do you love humanity?' And, stuffing her nose in her skirt to protect her from the stench, she answered him for the third time: 'Yes'."

Both women laughed and laughed up the hill, their hoots muffled by their petticoats.

On the sidewalks, at intervals, small fires burned under pots of oil frying acarajé, the bean cakes sacred to the orisha Yansá. A barefoot boy of eleven charged through the crowd carrying an iron pot of boiling oil. The revellers he pushed through, alarmed at the disaster awaiting the slightest trigger—a dancing elbow, a shift of weight in the throng—shouted angrily at him.

Francisca, like a handful of others, stopped to watch a dancer in a snow-white dress. The cells of the dancer's body seemed to have been marinated in the music from birth so her slightest movement released a rich, aromatic energy. She passed the rhythm through her body, letting it play with her head, touch the smile on her lips, slip down to flow like liquid between her shoulders, chase languidly round her rib cage, fall gently to circle her hips, and finally slip into her legs, wobbling them inward with a grace that stunned the onlookers.

An odd image came to Francisca as she watched: That American journalist, Emma Marr, whose head was always ordering her body around like it knew better, denying her sleep and even a timely glass of water and certainly, play. But there were those few moments at the party in Bangladesh at the population conference when Francisca had jiggled her samba-saturated arms against the American. Emma's stiff limbs loosened and the samba flowed through them. Remembering, Francisca stepped out of the circle around the liquid dancer and moved down the street, smiling to herself.

She looked up. Terror and awe filled her. Something was happening to the sky. Some huge upheaval was taking place in the natural world. The sky, which should have been black and filled with the Southern Cross, was becoming light. She stared in confusion.

What …? Wonder at the mystery of the planet made every cell in her body alert. Awe drugged her.

She grabbed a passing reveller and pointed upwards.

"The sky," she said. "Something is happening to the sky!"

His eyes followed her finger.

"Dawn," he said calmly, and danced away.

Dawn. What a fascinating explanation. She never would have thought of it. Of course she'd kept no track of time. There was no reason to. What possible difference could it make if it were 10 p.m. or 4 a.m.? You wouldn't stop dancing just because of what a watch said.

Now, the sun. She could see it peeking behind the hill. It was slowly lighting into visibility far away from her, and with the emerging hill, crowds of people dancing on it became visible as well. From darkness into light: Dancers on a hill.

Her heart suddenly reached out in deep connection to these people she'd been dancing with for six days and nights in the streets of Salvador, people still dancing in the dawn. If it were dawn, that meant it was Ash Wednesday and carnival was over and Lent was here. But still the people danced, now with sunbeams falling on their radiant faces. They wouldn't go home and do penance. They were supposed to fast. To give up joys and pleasures. To fall on their knees and bow their heads. But they weren't ready. They were too filled with orishas to be good Catholics.

Hundreds and thousands of people in the dawn. This was no 'population explosion' as the North American men had called it at the conference in Bangladesh, but a 'protoplasm explosion'. That's what they were, all of them dancing in the streets: protoplasm. That's how it looked from the heavens—one being, one mass of protoplasm oozing down one street, changing shape to flow into another street, spreading through the city, some parts of the protoplasm briefly flaring up in anger or violence and that was fine too, that was part of it, the vibrant red of anger as stunning in the bouquet of emotions as the flaming yellow of love. She was one with all these others—feeble, bent, about-to-depart or newly arrived and yet tender; long black dreadlocks or short blond curls; one-legged or hunchbacked; crazed, calculating, or tranced. She saw the joy radiating from the multi-headed faces of the protoplasm, felt that same joy streaming forth from her own, and knew that they were one being.

A protoplasm explosion: rich, vibrant, succulent, juicy, pulsating. No silence of a sterilized womb here but the music of rowdy life pushed out of women's dark interior to dance on the streets of Salvador.

Her whole body overflowing with love for these people, she began to dance it, and her dancing was so spirit-filled, revellers she passed by beamed at her, laughed in response to her joy, reached out and touched her with affection.

A single file of sambaing carnival jumpers, each person holding onto the waist of the person in front, snaked through the crowd near Francisca, their faces radiating joy. Suddenly she felt a great force pushing against her, a swirl of violence.

Francisca had seen such sudden squalls of violence before. Maybe some started when pickpockets launched fights to divert attention while they filched the change revellers kept for beer and the bacteria-laden snacks. Some man would shove or slug another and the violence pushed into the crowd as people screamed and tried to stay on their feet and not be trampled to the ground by the force of the moving crowd. Usually, as suddenly as it began, it stopped, because the thief danced on. The violent squall would be immediately followed by another single file of exuberant revellers sambaing their sweat-glistened bodies through the mass of humanity, the sudden contrast between terror and joy taking your breath away.

But this time wasn't usual. This time, before the squall passed, in the confusion of the screams, a man costumed as an Apache in a feathered headdress, fringed shirt, with a loincloth suspended from a string around his waist, approached Francisca. Standing behind her, he raised his hatchet and brought it down on her head.

Francisca dropped to the sidewalk, blood running out of her, the trickles forming lines, some intersecting as if in a genogram tracing her descendants. She was the ancient goddess Tiamat, felled in Babylonian antiquity by the god Marduk. Now Marduk, in his carnival guise, was slipping into the crowd.

All her life Francisca had felt the work of guarding women from Marduk was on her. But it wasn't all on her or on Khaleda or Suzanne. She felt that now. It wasn't all on the women around the world she had worked with for decades, many of them gathering most recently in Bangladesh: the feminists resisting brutal contraceptives; resisting forced sterilization of black and brown women; resisting the trafficking in women as surrogate mothers; resisting the reduction of women to raw supplies of eggs and uteri; resisting genital mutilation. No, the resistance wasn't all on them.

As the blood ran out of her, Francisca could imagine the world without her in it. She could sense that the blood seeping from her wound were the lines of women who would be born after her and carry on this work. There were such women coming into this world. The shining ones: passionate, empathic, brilliant, courageous.

Her blood, splattered on the sidewalk, would spill through the generations. The shining young women likely would never know of her. But she would be watching over them, responding to their calls and, ever so benevolently, haunting them.

Apostrophe to Anger

PRAMILA VENKATESWARAN

Anger is not a bad word
—Myisha Cherry

You live in a woman who is on the verge of erupting
        over so many little hurts
some might call them silly,
as she does to soothe herself.
                    But you
shake her awake.

At first the husband's put-downs and mind games itch,
            then quieten, only to flare up
when he accuses her of falling short
                of something. Or, when
he says, "I never said that.
You must be imagining it." She doubts herself, but feels
              you sharp and sure,
like a burn of whisky or a pop of tart berry.

This is how you come home to her,
in the dingy interior where the only light that sparks
is when her children laugh: You shock her into seeing
        a burst of neon signs screaming "Warning, warning!"
        when her husband gaslights her.

If you were a different emotion, like sadness
or fear, she would not believe in herself.
			She would find shelter
			in the dank rut of survival.

			But you jab and prod,
inject her will to surge into action,
		to seek refuge for herself and her children,
			so they are free to think and to live.
			Soon, she finds solace in your mauling.

Still, you wound kindly. You cauterize.
She will bid you *au revoir*
			for you have ignited her resolve.

The thickness of choice

FIONA PLACE

She is in the thick of it;
a vagina hot throbbing,
a vagina blood seeping,
nipples milk oozing.

She collapse flies night after night,
Collapse dreams night after night
and page scouring the alphabet,
pick playfully pronounces *this*, or *that* name,
this or *that* moniker from the pocket book guide's
A to Z list.

What about Camilla? she joshes,
or perhaps, seasonal Summer?
What about — ? What about — ?
School mothers cheerfully chastise her,
that baby named yet?
They mock protest,
mock protest as she daily shepherds
her twins and their backpacks
into the kindergarten classroom.

Sachin and Alexis were named instantly,
named within hours of their first lustful cries.
No book needed.
It was as though (*she would later say*),
as though they'd each arrived with their names
lovingly forehead etched.

But with this baby there seems
no name in sight.
None.
What's more this baby
seems immune
to the nightly barrage,
the late evening musings
of A to Z.

It's ridiculous, she jest flounces.
Absurd.
Four weeks to lodge a name
and we've already marched
aimless through three.
How, she wonders, how could twenty-one nights,
each thick with names, each thick with possibilities,
just fizzle flame out?

Then, a night shy of the deadline,
exhausted, nipple weary,
and still uterus blood clot expunging,
she clasps the tiny feet resting against
a receding stomach, marvels at the tiny mouth
milk emptying a hard breast,
and blurt announces she might've got it.

She is hesitant.
It is uncommon.
Precious.
Passed on from a great aunt.
It was her sister's middle name,
a childhood loss still grieved,
a childhood grave still left unseen.
Would it be a burden or a blessing?
Should she even mention it?

Now it's just an idea, she prefaces, just
a suggestion, and it's not in the book
she warn tells husband Gerard.
He waits.
Waits gently.
'Til, tenderly stroking her daughter's forehead,
she softly sounds out *Je-ru-sa*,
her intended gift.

I think it's beautiful, he responds,
you've struck gold, she'll carry it well.
And those mothers will get off my case
she replies, instantly regretful she's swept
away the soul of the moment.
Swept swift away the loving arch of the moment.

From within the thick of it,
from within the fierce furnace
of post birth bodily change,
she finally strive carves out her last slice
of motherhood, those three small syllables welcoming
her second daughter, welcoming baby Jerusa
into her now child finished family.

The Treehouse

JACQUE DUFFY

The tightening in my tummy as my eyes followed the trunk up,

up,

forever

up,

into that treemountain made vomit come into my mouth.

I swallowed it

down

and felt nostrilburn.

Stinging. Hot. Nasty.

Branches extending forever, a Hindu Goddess waving.
Sunlight barely making it through the canopy of arms and
waving fingers. Except minute points, where, if positioned just
right, they could blind a person. I immediately decided they
were the perfect adult foil, laser pointers, just like the movies.

It was those laser pointers I had to reach.
A task that could be my undoing.

Defeat.

Drown in shame.

Bigger than the windmill. The Candlenut tree was giantnormously tall … and wide, there was no chance of me monkeyslithering, wrapping my arms and legs around the smooth leather-like bark if I lost my footing. Slipped. Fumbled. Grazesoninnerthighs. Ouch. Another adult foil. Keep out. Grownups were nowhere near as nimble and as daring brave courageous as kids, except maybe my uncle is brave enough; he flies helicopters and wrestles buffalo with shotguns. High up and brave.

My uncle, your father. You.

You.

You, I want to make proud.

You I want to be around.

You and those boys from your school rocketed up the invisisticks of timber nailed to the silver cream bark as though it was a ladder. Staircase. Walk in the park. I worried I would make a dicklessloser of myself, get stuckfallbreak, giving you wonderboys another reason not to include me. Not able to keep up. I rememberflicted worse pain by pinching parts of myself till tears came and left, glassy-eyed supervision. I had to do this. I wanted to do this. I would do this.

Heart racing Phar Lap they're off, thump thump thump. Throatburn.

I still feel the splinter ignored till festered; no way was I letting you know my skin was softer than yours. Delicate. Girlish.

Up I went. Monkeyslither grasping invisisticks.

Looking

down at the miniscule grass and rocks that appeared between my outstretched wide apart legs as I strugglemadeit from the treeclimb horror to the roof it seemed insurmountably

far

away.

My legs and I were a bit jellified.

I remember being so impressed, so impressed, as we stood together on the roof.

I was one of the boys.

I was with you.

You could be proud of me, your girlcousinshouldbeaboy.

So high up. A wonderboy too.

You showed off your sky saturated club house secret hideaway, your world, enchanting. Exhilaration, I was the first girl, only girl, to see it.

Ripples beneath our feet. Corrugated and waving.

Colourbond clouds and rainbows surrounding and moving through our playground. The air in our laserlit sanctuary was a kind of opalescent yellowgreenblueseethrough sparkle, it glowed like a bejewelled golden crown. The glow's sensation made me feel amazing, unrestricted, and unconquerable. I was home. In an extraordinary away from normal bedtime dullness and rules place. I was with you and so high, moonshot, comet-tailed, meteoric. Together we had arrived in a new ecosphere. Globe cut in half. We were in the core. Centre of the world. New world. Dreamlike world. I sensed l had become the artsy and beautiful fairy princess returned to her people after the long-forgotten-about amnesiesque absence—I wouldn't risk telling you, remind you I was a girl. Different. Not accepted.

Risk expulsion.

Risk eviction.

Risk not being with you.

First girl only girl in the clique. Inaugural. Formalities must be completed by the maiden to be admitted. The boy treehouse secret club world. Initiation. You quietly apologise, gently, so friends won't hear. I don't care too much. Take it in my stride. I want this. Entirely happy to earn my place. My acceptance, dog poo smear nearby door handles, let down random car tyres flatasatack. Rotten eggs in swimming pools. Indiscriminate. I do not live close, your neighbours would never guess, no idea, your idea, it was me. So proudofme. I did it.

Neverland we had our own. Elation. We were the tiny specks inside the giant leafdiscoball laserlights shooting everywhichway enclosed, hidden from normallife. Magnificence. I spun and spiralled on the inside, flip flip heartbeats. Enclosed in a giant security colander, laserpointprotected, cone of comfort not silence. Birdsong flyingwild tame loud energetic. Singing for peace. Singing for joy. Singing for us.

Further formality. Ceremony. Celebration ritual number one observed. Not my job newcomer. Newcomer, novice, tenderfoot, beginner can participate in the many to follow. Round hard treenuts, hurting tenderfeet watchout. I watched you cut open, peel tops, ceremoniously light and place. Wide candlenut circle like fireflies surrounding a pile of crunchy collected leaf and stick matter also lit … a floating fire, burning ball, stars, constellation, Milky Way, universe. High up in the rippled sky, the small sun. Our sun. I was in heaven. Your heaven. Our heaven.

Dark green verytop branches of the gazillion aged mulberry tree peeked over the edge into the protected corrugated world. Celebration ritual two. Devouring. Gobbling. Face painting and gorging on the tippytop fruit we feasted a royal and colourful feast. Tiny beads of flavour. Purple grubs. Fingers mouths chindribbles war paint or in my case discreet princess markings, tattooed patterns verypretty. Till the tummy tightening happened again, urges, crossed legs crossed fingers. In the firefly-filled shade of the candlenut tree I wanted to pee. Too scaredanxiousfearful to climb down alone and spoil special moments. Bailout. Leave go disappear convert to uninitiated. Not that I told you, I figured I could hold on. Sweat it out.

Until.

Celebration ritual three.

You and your school boy friends lined up on the edge of our rippled world and drew swords yellow spray cut the air four perfect arcs, as one you all turned faces to look at me. Urge me to join the ritual. Cajole. Coerce.

How?

How, I could not arc?

I could not stand and arc.

I could hardly stand with my legs straight straining. Bursting. Agony. Another initiation … How was I to do that? Now. Then. Ever.

Villain tummy. Burning. Pleading looks your way. Unable to hold it in any longer. Red-faced, full-bellied. In pain. Wanting your faces to turn away whilst I squatbalanced my bottom extruding over the edge of the rippled world.

I remember peeing relief. Wee a river. Flood a puddle. Noisy drumming down in the regular world far below. I remember.

Being unable. Unable to   stop   the flow river cascade.
We heard Frieda, our grandmother, the only person I could
possibly love more than you   call   my   name.

She stood below, her face aimed in my general direction,
fortunately, luckily, thank God, the laser pointers had her
blinded. She was trying to see inside the giant leafdiscoball
laserlights shooting everywhichway enclosed, hidden from
view.

Slowly.

Deliberately.

Torturously.

Heart flip flip. She raised her arm to shade her beautifully
wrinkled lovefilled heartbursting crystal blue eyes. I felt them.
Her eyes, reverse lasers as they focused on my uncovered
bottom sunlit rainbow protruding from the rippled world
edge. Exposed. Guilty. Shamed. I saw myself telescopically
mirrored in her eyes, embarrassed. Loathing myself wishing
for invisability, a new self. A time machine. She looked away.
Horrified. Her, and I, and you, the three of us, horrified.
Disturbed. Mystified. What had she discovered found
stumbled upon, disappointed in her granddaughter. Princess.

Time

Slowed

I remember

feeling the blood leave my face. Only mulberry tattoos and
saltwatergoggles remained. Losing balance dizzy wobbleshriek.
Swirling in the worst possible way. Express elevator. Jolted
as you grabseized me and stopped me topplefalling to the
earth below. Hero. Mine. You held me tight. I look. Dismay
written in mulberry on your face. Your schoolboy friends

laughing. At me at you. Pointing. Ankle undies wet. Bare rainbow bottom unprotected no more secrets. I had spoiled everything. Charmless. Unpleasant. Death to the princess. End of acceptance into your laserlit sanctuary with its opalescent yellowgreenblueseethrough sparkle. Never again to feel unconquerable. Never again to be free in the extraordinary land far from normalness. No more would I be with you so high and moonshot. No longer could I visit the ecosphere. Globe cut in half. Centre of the world. Dreamlike world.

Failed.

I was the Dicklessloser.

WishIwasdead.

Should have topplefallen.

Defeated.

Lost forever.

With my heart peeled like an apple and slick eyed saltwatersupervision

I descended

from the

rippled world edge.

Up was easier than down.

Except I no longer felt fear to descend alone.

No fear of making things worse.

Already defeated and brokensplit what else could go wrong. Turn bad. Go off.

Grandma Frieda.

Disappointed in me. Sad. Speechless. Silent.

Until.

One look. Eye spy, gentle inspection and transfer of dread anxiety loss defeat hurt from me to her … No more Grandma reverse laser eyes. I had not let Grandma Frieda down.
She held grannyhugsqueezed comforted. She knew. I knew.
We knew. There would be discussion later. There would be trouble, me especially. Lesson learned. Debutant princesses of laserlit sanctuaries with opalescent yellowgreenblueseethrough sparkle do not squatbalance over edges of rippled worlds.

Keep Telling

MARION MOLTENO

I watch my four-year-old granddaughter scream unstoppably for no reason that any of us can fathom, except of course there is a reason that we all know. Her mother is ill. Whatever we might say to reassure her, it's obvious that we're all worried, and she doesn't want either her dad or a visiting grandma looking after her. So whatever we suggest triggers a crisis.

This time Dave, her dad, is dealing with it, or attempting to. I remove myself from the kitchen so that I'm not watching. Not that they're noticing me. Were my own daughters ever like this? I remember tantrums, but this feels different. Was I? I have no memory of it. But I never had these pressures. Perhaps my own mother was, when they told her that *her* mother was ill and had to be left to rest?

What will Lisa remember of all this, in years to come?

Only what life flung at her, I imagine, not how others saw her react.

Dave leaves for work and will be gone two days. That's a relief—there are tensions there that I am not party to, and don't want to be. None of us are tension-free but it feels simpler with one fewer person generating them. Jessie is upstairs, trying to rest, trying to pretend she is not following every sound we make, anxious that I'm not doing it right.

I'm trying to get some breakfast into the child, without making an issue of it. She is expert at delay tactics. Currently she is arranging cutlery in patterns. "Keep telling," she says as she considers where to place a teaspoon. *Telling* means stories. Any stories. The story-monster in her brain requires a constant backdrop of words to get her through the tedious tasks adults insist on—another two spoonfuls of porridge, brushing teeth.

I give up on breakfast and suggest that we pack up her Sylvanians before we set off. This nearly sparks another crisis. These small dressed-animals, always in conventional happy families (mother, father, two children), move in her fertile imagination in a story-drama which, thankfully, keeps her focused on things other than Jessie upstairs. But the game is never finished—we are interrupting it to go to the park—so the Sylvanians have to stay *right there*, filling up the floor. If she were my child I would provide a large tray on which Sylvanian stories could happen, which could be lifted out of the way at meal times. But she is not; and it's too late now.

I manage to extract her long enough to persuade her wriggly limbs to accommodate shoes, gloves, coat, woolly hat. At the door I pause to check that I have my Five Things without which I do not leave houses. Keys, purse, travel pass, phone—What *is* the fifth?

"I can't even count up to five," I say, waiting for Number Five to arrive in my increasingly erratic memory.

"Glasses," she says. "Your right glasses."

"That's it, long-distance glasses. Clever girl."

We set off, down the pavement.

"Do you have dementia?" she asks.

"I don't think so."

"Dementia is when you can't remember things, like glasses."

"True, but I don't think it's that bad yet. It's when you can't remember what glasses are for, even when you find them."

Her matter-of-factness delights me. She is a child who *needs* to know, who will imagine if you don't tell her, and whose antennae are always out to check that she has been told the whole truth —though she is consistently told much more of it than most children her age. Certainly more than I told my children. Vastly more than I was ever told.

Is her mother going to die? The question hovers, unspoken. Jessie is several weeks into the chemotherapy, and they've been reading a book called *Mummy's Lump*. It's all going to be OK, the world tells her, but she slices through assumed cheeriness, reads expressions on faces, tones of voice. For the first few days after each bout of treatment, Jessie is not the kind of mum Lisa is used to—vital, spontaneous, fun. Even her voice has changed. It's the medicine, we explain. It makes her very tired, and she has to rest, but it's making her better. Jessie summons a reduced version of her old self whenever she's with Lisa, but she can't hide how much of an effort it is.

We cross the road, passing little front gardens in this row of identical terraced houses. A family of gnomes in one, then one with pebbles and grasses. A few brave pansies still producing colour in the next.

"Keep telling," she says.

Jessie just makes stories up to order, has been doing it since Lisa was an infant. Difficult for anyone else to live up to.

"Why don't we just look at things along the way? Like the different kinds of garden we're passing."

"I can look *and* listen."

"I'm no good at making up stories."

"Then tell a real story."

Tell a real story … Why have I not found a way to package for this voracious child all the stories I carry of earlier childhoods? Her mother's, my own? I dredge around, and come up with the time I had my tonsils out. Perhaps that will have an Ancient

History curiosity—children don't seem to have their tonsils out these days. Then I get to the dramatic bit, that after I was home the bleeding didn't stop and I had to go back to hospital in an ambulance—and I stop just in time. This is *not* what we want, a story about operations not going right. I sidetrack quickly to school, how we had to knit socks for our fathers, which was totally unfair because my dad had bigger feet than anyone else's.

Childhoods are not simple. I can't think of any stories anodyne enough.

My mother ... hers is the only one in the line of childhoods I can trace who had to deal with what Lisa is dealing with now. But I certainly can't tell that story because it has the wrong ending.

We had just one photo of my mother's mother, Agnes, a young woman in Edwardian dress, standing at the side of a piano, her hand resting on it. I loved that photo. There was about the as-yet-unmarried Agnes a simple, open loveliness, a quality of awareness, as if she were listening, absorbed. Her eyes look steadily at the camera—*at me*, I as a child was convinced. My mother had no memory of her. There was a picture in her mind, she said, but she wondered if it was a product of a child's imagination, filling the absence? It was a basement, with windows that looked out at people's feet on the pavement. That must have been Edinburgh, and she would have been about three, younger than this child. I try to picture her, dressed as little girls were then, in a long pinafore dress. Somewhere, shadowy in the background, was a young woman, gentle, always tired. I can't think of that now without a concerned grandmother's eye. What was happening to that three-year old child while her father was at work and her mother exhausted from TB? Who was caring for her? A grandmother? An aunt? A neighbour? Whoever did it, it must have been loving care, for it's in those first years that we learn to love. The receiving of love, which is the wellspring of the giving.

And what would her father have told her, after her mother was gone? She remembered, from later, that he didn't like to be reminded of that time, so perhaps she learnt not to ask. But she knew things without being told. She knew that he had wanted to take her to a warmer place, and had a terror of her getting ill. Years later she had only to shiver for him to give her money and say, "Go and buy yourself a good coat." She felt guilty when she took it, she said, for she knew he was always short of money.

All the stories I can think of turn out to be full of traps for the unsuspecting. Things going on in adult lives that ricochet, destabilise, whether anyone explains or not.

We have reached the park. I can stop searching for stories. Lisa is off, on a swing. I push. This is easy.

"Higher," she insists.

I watch her legs kick against the sky. Momentarily she is simply a child, full tilt into the present moment. I am trailing back, counting to five, from Agnes, to my mother, to me, to Jessie, this child—

Who has suddenly had enough of swings.

The air is cold on our faces as we walk home to the promise of hot chocolate, in a house where Lisa will remember once again that her mother is upstairs resting and shouldn't be disturbed.

As we turn the corner, she says, to ward off that moment, "Keep telling."

I have no energy to make anything up. My mother's childhood has been in my mind, so that's what Lisa gets. The safe parts, dredging memory for things I must have been told when I was this child's age and asked for stories. How she started off in Scotland but then she and her dad went on a big adventure, going on a ship across the ocean to a country thousands of miles away, where the winters were never as cold as in Scotland. And how they came back once, when she was eleven, and stayed in the house where her mother had grown up. Her Grandpa was full of jokes and teasing, and had a flute that stood behind the parlour door, which he sometimes played for her. There was a long garden at the back of the house that dropped down to the river that ran through the town, so her Grandma didn't let her play there. She slept in a little bedroom with a picture called Cherry Ripe above the bed. She wished passionately that it belonged to her, but she never asked for it …

By bedtime it's a toss-up which of the three of us is the most tired. Jessie looks utterly drained, her face an unnatural yellow from all the drugs they've been pumping into her, her still-young forehead creased with anxiety. She insists on doing the bedtime story herself. Lisa has worn herself out—constant activity, turbulent emotion. Now she cuddles as she listens, and will fall asleep—eventually—in the place of ultimate safety, next to her mum. But it won't be for a while. She resists letting go. And why not, when you can't be sure what it is you're letting go of?

And I? I'm suddenly feeling my age, from negotiating unexpected roles. From being a grandmother to a firecracker who one minute lights up in creativity, and then suddenly is a whirring wheel of confusion. From preparing meals not in my own home, where I don't know which cupboard anything goes in, and trying to tidy up when I can't move for Sylvanians. From being mother to a daughter whom I have loved forever, and forever will, and who, now that she is ill, I can do so little to help.

There isn't a spare room, so I settle myself to sleep in Lisa's little room. Jessie has decorated the walls with delicate stencil paintings of trailing vines and birds. I remember Jessie's first room, where I'd painted one wall with blackboard paint so she could draw on the walls as much as she liked. And back from there to the room I grew up in, that had a climbing rose outside the window that scratched against it when the wind blew; and a tall wardrobe that came from an aunt, with a big drawer at the bottom where our cat once produced a litter of kittens among my knickers. And back further still, to the little room in Cupar with a picture of Cherry Ripe, probably long since on a rubbish heap.

If I'm lucky, in the morning Lisa will come and climb into this bed with me, and I'll keep telling, about that long line of child rooms, small places of safety. And while we're laughing about the kittens in my knickers, we'll forget, both of us, to be worried.

My Cup Runneth Over

ANNE OSTBY

She reads the poem slowly and feels it sink deep into her. Settling in her stomach, between her ribs, the words forming layer after layer until they fill her up all the way to her throat. They lie there at the bottom of her vocal chords, aching to burst out, in longing or in protest.

> *Light the expensive candles on a Tuesday.*
> *Use the nice china for a cup of coffee with yourself.*
> *Don't wait for the house to be clean; dust has its own beauty.*

Sure, sure. She rubs her tired eyes with one hand. Lets her gaze slide across the crumbs on the counter, tries to focus on the pale sunlight outside the window that should have been washed. Tries to summon appreciation for the beauty in the dust bunnies behind the radiator.

The candleholder is burnt down to four red stumps, the base full of melted wax. Let it go; it's only appearances, it doesn't count. She opens the bottom dresser drawer and pulls out the aromatherapy candle she's been saving. The tissue paper wrap smells of dust and lily-of-the-valley. Because you're worth it, she says to herself. The cream-colored candle won't fit in the holder; it points at her with an accusatory wick.

There are no tasks to check off the list this morning. The phone doesn't ring. *Don't struggle to find calm, the heart has its own peace.* The silence when no voices are heard, the vacuum of the walls around her, the ticking of the kitchen clock that echoes through her body. The heart's peace, where is it? The calm that fills the soul when everything unimportant falls away. The golden zen that frees the mind and raises her gently and generously up above the humming of the washing machine. But the heart isn't calm! It cries out to be heard. To bleed and ache and be broken!

Don't wait for the perfect partner; enjoy the arms that embrace you. She and Paul—they're doing all right. The mortgage paid off, their little cabin in the mountains. He's away a lot: work, volunteering, political commitments. She doesn't mind. Being alone gives her freedom. Freedom to be nothing. Why won't that snide remark from nearly twenty years ago stop stinging?

Lina was thirteen when she tossed it out, at the start of the unwavering resentment of her parents that would mark most of her teenage years. She had stood there with the envelope in her hand, the university diploma that proved Molly J. Rutland (now Winters) had earned a master's degree in chemistry, with honors. After Lina, and then the twins Adam and Aaron showed up in quick succession, she had been glad to have the part-time job at the pharmacy and co-workers who changed shifts with her when the kids got sick with sore throats and endless ear infections. Adam's asthma keeping her up at night, Aaron's unexplainable stomach aches with every slight change to his daily routine. All the more painful, then, when her daughter had stood there with Molly's diploma in her hand and scorn curling the corners of her mouth: "You have a *master's degree*, mom? God! And you decided to become … *nothing?*"

A splash of cold coffee is left at the bottom of the mug on the table. The glaze on the handle is chipped, worn down by her sleepy thumb over hundreds of mornings at the kitchen table.

Work, there was always work to be done. The house they bought was a fixer-upper, she was on her hands and knees grouting tiles with her pregnant belly dragging against the floor mere weeks before Lina arrived. At the same time her father was ill, the excruciatingly slow stomach cancer and her mother insisting on nursing him at home: "It's the least I can do."

Birth and postpartum and death and burial, the next few years involved every feeling on the spectrum and ate up all her energy. And it was never-ending. Her mom who wanted to move into an apartment, the childhood home that had to be emptied, her brother who probably imagined he was being helpful as he sat there with his busy job a day's journey away. "Just throw it all out," he said. "I don't want any of it."

Work, work, all the invisible work. Doctor's appointments to make, clothes to handwash. Flowers to put in vases, scrapes to put band-aids on. Divorcing friends to comfort. Groceries to buy. Christmas presents and potlucks and drains to be cleaned. Days that rush by. Tuesdays and Thursdays filling themselves up while nothing ever gets done.

World's best mom, the optimistic letters along the rim of the coffee mug proclaim. Is she really? She got it for Mother's Day a few years ago, a fun little trinket alongside the flowers her children always remember to send. She'd been happy, even a little touched. From nothing to *world's best mom*, surely that's a big jump?

She quickly reminds herself of everything she has to be grateful for. Lina's newly opened photography studio. Adam the electrician, Aaron with a steady job as a nurse. *Don't wait for your kids to be perfect; let them shine with their own light.* Why can't she get that damn poem out of her head!

Use the nice china for a cup of coffee with yourself. Behind the glass doors in the china cabinet, the gold-rimmed Wedgwood set sits untouched and unapproachable. Does coffee taste better in a golden cup? Make you feel better about yourself? The old mug sits alone on the edge of the table. No half-empty milk glasses alongside it, no untippable sippy cups with lead bottoms.

God, how guilty she had felt about them afterwards. Were they dangerous? Had her kids ingested toxic chemicals because she'd been too lazy to clean spilled milk from an upturned cup? Damage to the bone marrow and nervous system, stunted growth and learning disabilities. Lina wasn't reading properly until well into third grade, was there a connection there? The work of worry, endless and exhausting, that was always hers, too.

Serve yourself in the nice china. She knows it's somewhere in the basement, the mug with the lumpy bottom. Big wide rim, that's the way it was supposed to be back when everyone was taking pottery classes, spinning mugs with green or blue glaze. That was a gift too, for—was it her 25th birthday? Her 30th? From Evie, her friend who did the unthinkable and chose no husband, no kids, no mortgage or retirement fund. Evie, who chose art and secondhand clothes and scrimping and saving instead, who still lived in a collective when she was approaching 40. The last she'd heard of her was something about a stipend to go to Portugal. Wonder what Evie's drinking from now, she thinks and lifts *World's best mom* to her lips. Envisions a beachfront restaurant, loose clothing, a head thrown back in laughter. Fingers with chunky silver rings holding a glass, thick and opaque, wine shimmering dark red, nearly black. How little wine she herself has drunk! No, sorry, I have to drive home. I have to call it quits, the kids get up so early. I have to … I need to … no thanks.

She finds her reading glasses and tucks her hair behind her ears. Reads the pat-on-the-shoulder, love-yourself platitudes yet again. *Don't wait around for world peace; let go! Breathe peace in and out with every breath.* The words drift across the page in a breeze of soft harp strumming and the fragrance of lilacs. A smiling woman, young, with flowing hair, who lets her inner peace radiate out into the world. Be in the now. Peace in the moment. She hears her own choppy breath, impatient, boots scraping against the pavement. There is no world peace.

No inner enlightenment connecting us all in meditative unity. Let go—who the hell can let go? As long as Rohingya women in Myanmar watch their babies thrown into flaming fires while laughing soldiers rape their daughters? As long as girls' schools in Afghanistan are still closed? As long as abortion laws in the US are being reversed and taxi drivers can be punished for driving women to the clinic? No. Zen has its time and place, but it's not here and it's not now.

She stands up. The poem's words throb loud and scornful in her ears. *Don't wait to accomplish something grand, be grateful just to live every day.* No! She's never accomplished anything grand. Never made a scientific discovery. Never uttered a memorable quote that will live forever. But is that all that's left—counting the days, hanging in there, getting through it? *The irreversible has already happened, and I survived.* Is that supposed to be a comfort? A softening, a conciliatory assurance that things can't get any worse? She wants more than just to survive. Much more! *I no longer wait for recognition.* Hell yes! She is still waiting for recognition, that's for damn sure. She's 59 years old, and it's not over yet!

She isn't breathing peace in and out of her body. She isn't dancing in complete harmony with the moon. Molly J. Winters (née Rutland) wants recognition. Not for the street that's never been named after her, but for 31 years of runny noses and grumpy customers and explanations of how to use ear cleaners and wart removers. She wants appreciation for all the birthday parties planned, all the errands run and groceries shopped, all the phone calls made so the days and years would go round.

Use the finest china when you sit alone at the table. She walks down to the basement. The boxes are unmarked, but she finds the right one. Her fingers recognize it through layers of bubble wrap and tape. Roughly formed with a crooked handle, but the color is just the way she remembers it. Bluish green, probably a little darker than the ocean just beyond the beachfront restaurant that might be called *Brisa do mar*. She drops the bubble wrap on the floor and lifts the mug to her mouth. Inhales the scent of the hot tea, assam or darjeeling, jasmine tea in tiny pearls.

She balances it on its saucer back into the kitchen. It's been in the box long enough, and doesn't have a single letter around the rim.

Molly J. Winters. Woman, 59. Her cup runneth over.

Skoteino Cave

COLEEN CLARE

Tessa watches five excited women dismount their small tour bus and set out for Skoteino Cave. Grey clouds surround slate mountains looming over hidden gaps in the earth. Chilled to the bone, the travellers clutch jackets as they trudge along a goat track.

As their guide on this pilgrimage, Tessa informs them Skoteino Cave has five levels of cavernous rooms. A snake-like coil of climbing gear nestles in the waving grass. Faith, the eldest pilgrim, eyes it warily. Pale-faced, she mutters, "How deep did you say it was?"

Upbeat, Tessa responds. "It is about thirty metres wide and sixty metres deep. It has a great history from Minoan times and is called the Cave of Goddess Skoteina of the Dark and Fertility."

Faith is seventy plus and has a gammy knee; she is full of trepidation as she takes a tentative step through the deep aperture into the gloom. She grabs on to the edge of a jagged rock—it wobbles alarmingly and grazes her hand.

Her younger companions—Zoe, Hira, Rita and Kerryn—clamber in and edge past her. A wave of sadness washes over Faith; it is hard to accept there is so much she cannot do now. Her mind flashes back to the mountains she climbed in her youth. She shakes herself, physically and mentally. She is proud she has made it inside this unique cave, even if only to sit and meditate.

Tessa has other ideas. "Come on, Faith—you can make it further down."

Their descent is slow, small rocks dislodge, bounce from level to level and crash into the chasm below.

Faith squeaks, "I think I should stop here!"

"Okay. There will be a safe spot soon where you can sit. You can be our halfway sentinel and await our return." Tessa's voice is warm and reassuring.

Faith stumbles and her foot sends a large rock clunking down the path. "That's it! I am staying right here." She edges her bottom on to a small rock ledge.

Tessa reaches out a hand to Faith. "Are you sure? That spot does not look big enough for your bottom. We could go down a bit further and find a more accommodating rock."

"This is fine." Faith is not moving. "Truly, I am not going another inch. I will wait here."

"All right. You can have the company of these incredible stag things. Which one is up, and which one is down, Faith?"

"Stalactites are up, and stalagmites are down! Tites for top, mites for tiny on the bottom. That's what I used to tell my kids."

Because Faith is now sounding a little more cheerful, perched on her small rock, like a fledgling not ready to fly, Tessa moves briskly down to join the others.

Now alone, Faith suddenly feels unsteady. She cannot wait on this rock—she fears she is about to pitch into the blackness. She calls out to Tessa but her voice is a mere croak. Tessa does not hear her.

Gasping, Faith realises she did not get her torch back from Tessa; she is alone in total darkness. Tears fall, her calf muscles tighten into painful cords, her heart rhythm is irregular, her head is about to split. What if she falls? Images of her lifelong partner Cleo float before her eyes. Cleo, gone at sixty, monstered in half a year by pancreatic cancer.

Mice scatter as Tessa scurries to catch up with the others and share with them that this is her favourite cave in the whole of Crete. She waves her arms like the vanes of an ancient Cretan windmill, high above her and as far out to each side as she can stretch. She points to the rock formations that have emerged over thousands of years. "Look! There is the head of a woman. She was worshipped as a goddess. She sits above stored bones."

Zoe thinks the shadows are more like Hitchcock bird images than goddesses, or bats lurking waiting to shit on them. She races ahead, sure-footed, determined to be the first to reach the bottom. The others hesitate as they adjust to the velvet darkness.

Kerryn, the mystery woman of the group, is locked in her own memories. The air grows even colder, immense dark envelops her; she tugs her headscarf down and pulls her shawl around her. Shapeshifters are stalking her. All the suffering women she has worked with float around her; the clammy, smelly, press of rape invades her body. Her lips, fingers, toes, and uterus clench; her nails dig into her palms. Kerryn stifles her triggering thoughts with a steely prayerful focus, not to any male god, but to vengeful Kali.

A statuesque ghost in the shadows, Tessa instructs her pilgrims. "Stay silent. Each of you take a candle and light it from the mother candle. We will hold our candles aloft and chant. After which, on the count of three, we will blow the candles out and experience the utter darkness of this sacred cave."

Shudders shake Zoe; she feels her boundaries slip away. She knows the group thinks she is the young feisty one, rude and carefree. Only in the bar with Rita has she shared that she is a single mum taking a break from caring for her ten-year old daughter who has cerebral palsy. She lights her beeswax candle, protects the flame with her hand and concentrates on counting her breath in, and her breath out. She has taken this trip to regain her strength to care for Melody—she is not going to let herself be undone. The soft breath of her companions touches her bare skin.

"I feel like I am floating—I cannot feel my edges! Do I exist in this darkness?" Rita's voice breaks the silence. She longs to hold her lover Hira's hand, but it is not to be. Last night, sitting by the indigo ocean, watching a huge tangerine sun plop over the horizon, they had another fiery row about Rita's desire for a child, and Hira's determination to stay child-free.

Memories and experiences of the lives of each member of the pilgrimage are boiling over. Tessa gathers the group. "Now, we will call out into this sacred space the names of women who have inspired us." The chamber echoes with the names of women special to the pilgrims: the cavern fills with generations of female energy.

Kerryn lets out a long wail, followed by a soul-piercing litany of foreign names. Dragged from the very core of her being, the names roll on and on. Alarmed, the women gather around, but nobody touches Kerryn. Everyone breathes deeply and waits for the anguished flow to subside. Kerryn begins to quieten with a final gasp. "No more violence in our name—let it be undone!"

Tessa draws on all her inner strength to sustain Kerryn. She chants for the suffering of all women.

We go down—on a sleeping moon
We descend into darkness
We go down—blackness overwhelms us
We surrender.

Dark and Light
Light and Dark.

We climb on a crescent moon
We stagger up—light breaks
We know daylight will return
We accept.

Light and Dark
Dark and Light.

We are whole
We will survive
We will continue
We are born anew.

Tessa moves in to hold Kerryn, while Zoe, Hira and Rita join in the simple refrain. Voices rise floor by floor, fear melts, souls fly back to bodies.

High above, Faith freezes. She hears Kerryn wail. What is going on below her? She wonders if the darkness is releasing heartaches. She joins her voice to the comforting chant. Her fear of falling recedes. She sits like a statue and feels the sadness of her life. For the first time she sobs for the loss of Cleo. Her body relaxes, she waits.

Movement on the path heralds the return of Rita, followed by Hira.

"We are back Faith. Could you hear us? Can you turn round now? We have to go up a different way—it is too steep and crumbly where you are."

Anxious again, Faith's voice quavers out. "No, I can't turn Rita. It's too slippery."

Hira catches up with Rita. "What is the problem?"

"Faith is stuck, and she is frightened."

Hira, glad to have Rita talking to her again, assesses Faith's position. "Hi Faith. You have done so well; you are quite safe for the moment. Could you just hang on there a tick longer and I will come up and get you out?"

Faith's heart lifts, as the understanding and confidence in Hira's voice hits her.

"Thanks Hira. I have been so scared that I would fall. Do you think I can get out of here?"

"Of course, you can, Faith! What goes down must come up. Hang tight a second. I will come around behind you. You will lose sight of me for a minute, but Rita is standing there with the torch. In a sec I will be with you and get you back up top for a cuppa."

Faith thinks that she cannot possibly turn on this small ledge. Her hands are clammy, she rubs them on her damp jeans. She hears Hira moving in behind her. Each small movement makes her feel she is about to plunge to her death.

Hira speaks softly. "Faith, I am going to step down there beside you. There is plenty of room, but I am such a fatty you will need to move over to your left—just the tiniest bit if you please, Madam."

There is a small bounce as Hira lands beside Faith, wraps her arm around her and presses them both back into the rock. "Here we go babe—we need to turn and step up to Rita—up you go."

Faith is immovable.

Hira looks into the mask of fear on Faith's face. "I've got a much better idea. Why don't you lean into me; I will turn us both together and then we can edge up on our knees—a bit of a crawl."

An appalled look crosses Faith's face. Hira remembers that Faith has a crook knee that barely bends. "Shit!" Quickly she adds, "I don't mean bend that bad knee of yours, just a slide towards Rita and she will grab you quick smart."

Legs apart, Rita recalls her pilates classes. She breathes deeply into her diaphragm, braces her core, and takes the full weight of Faith's rag doll body as she slides toward her.

"Great work Faith—you are the best!" Rita struggles to regain her balance and the three women move inch by inch up the slope. Eventually the gradient lessens—they are back on the main track.

As Faith moves upwards under her own steam, Rita takes Hira's hand. "You did that so well, Hira." Hira squeezes her hand. Electricity races through her body, her heart fills with hot bubbles.

Shaken, but whole, the pilgrims regroup at the entrance to the cave. A sombre Kerryn joins them. Oblivious to Faith's drama, she has walked slowly back on the far side of the cave, locked in her inner world. In the abyss of the cave, she was assailed by memories of the thousands of women she had interviewed—the female rape victims of Bosnia. She died a thousand deaths as the names of the women were wrenched from her guts, and bloody memories washed through her.

Rita asks, "Where is Tessa?"

Kerryn is puzzled. "She passed me ages ago—she is up here somewhere."

At that moment, from outside the cave, Tessa sticks her head through the entrance. She invites the women to leave the darkness and step into the light. Faith steps up. "Let me go first please. That was amazing, scary but good. I feel stronger than I have for ages. It brought me closer to people I have lost."

Kerryn moves up next; she is calm. She steadies Faith as she climbs out.

Hira and Rita manage to exit still holding hands.

Tessa greets each pilgrim as they step into the light and announces to the world.

"And unto us a woman is born!"

Zoe bounds out last, rolls her eyes to the heavens and asks. "Where are we having lunch Tessa? We are all good now."

I would like to acknowledge Carol P. Christ who conducted scholarly pilgrimages through Minoan Crete using ritual and chant, one of which I was grateful to experience.

Coming of Age, Ready or Not

LAURIE ROSS TROTT

I require a shake up. A gentle lifting out of the gloomy sludge where my feet are planted, mindless plaque grouting my toes and laying a crusted salt, shell-like filament over the top, holding me firm to a spot that neither suits nor inspires.

I am as one who has walked aimlessly through the blossomed and patchouli oil-scented, leafy arcade of youth, meandered without direction into the weedy fields of middle age until woken with a short, sharp shock by the anxiety and overheated sleeplessness of unwelcome menopause; that time-clock terror that steals the juice from joints and, like a thief in the night, sucks out the firm smoothness of arm flesh and leaves creepy, crepey skin and flabby fadoobadas in its wake.

Asleep, I had watched the deconstruction of the bustling being that was my mother; witnessed her decline from Saturday night dancer to a constant keeper of a solitary, shaky beat and popping pills to try to step out of synch with Parkinson's tune.

But me? Old? Couldn't imagine it.

But what the? How now, this reality of grey hair, spider veins, arthritis and belly fat!

Nobody told me my eyebrows would disappear.

Nor prepared me for my grandchild's steely-eyed question, "What happened to your lips?"

My own eyes, once so keen and quick at spotting birds in the dim rainforest strata, grow salt rings around the irises and can no longer read a line of newsprint without magnification. But there, when I squint, I can just see, loitering on the periphery of awareness, a BIG SIX O that messes with my psyche and suggests I am heading like a lemming over the Niagara Falls on the border of time between now and then and into the grey, swampy seas of old age.

They say that 60 is the new 40. I breezed past 40, hoodwinked by fickle fashion into thinking I was fat in a size 12 and squeezing into little muffin top tummy trimmers and making a joke of playing veterans' hockey on the Perth Astroturf. I cast around for the feel of 40. And find myself mourning myself! Oh, Poor Me! My glory days are gone, I glibly quote, and duly note that I will never be this young again. I jokingly raise HRT with my doctor. She laughs, like I really am joking.

In a nod to youthful rebellion I quip that chardonnay will be my gentle companion into the quiet delusion and confusion of the mind's twilight zone; I shall shock them all, I fear, should I resent having to wear a nappy and my polite persona lets forth a string of invective more at home among a road gang than in the mouth of such a sweet old lady. But maybe not. Maybe by then the F-bomb will be well and truly a part of the general vocabulary.

Nae, I will not go gentle into that good night of purple persuasion, lawn bowls, ugly shoes and death notices.

But where is the passion to drive three score years from pain to gain? Where is the bold stare that meets me eye-to-eye in the mirror of my soul and sees not the large pores and furrowed, freckled skin reflecting decades of tropical summers, but rather, finds the ageing flesh too minor a given for distraction?

Where is the high-mindedness and intolerance for fools and time wasters that is the compensation for youth and its beauty having disappeared into the brief, dim dusk of a human life span?

Where is the gentle letting-go and self-acceptance?

I've managed to survive in this man's world and jostled with Gen X.

But the Millennials are a scary bunch; with them I feel anonymous, invisible, derisible, like it's 'boom-boom, game over' for the Boomer generation.

It's their world now and they are different. "You make me laugh," said one. With a smile. But my antenna was picking up a humouring, condescension frequency.

For the first time in my working life, I felt old.

So, I'm with Hamlet … "Oh, that this too, too-solid flesh would melt, thaw, and resolve itself into a dew …" —it is d-e-w as in overnight precipitation, but maybe it was a Shakespearean spelling mistake, maybe it should have been …

"Oh, that this too, too-solid flesh would melt, thaw, and resolve itself into … adieu …"

But then, where's the fun in that?

Elaine

For my sister Elaine on her 80th

PATRICIA SYKES

Elaine: 'Sun ray, shining light.' French variant of Helen.

You and I, how we fell into life like spiderlings on silk threads.
One breeze too many, or too less, and we'd have ended—
who knows where—as a shimmering accident.

Between them, Big Bang and God might claim the universe
but didn't we know, as we climbed and spun, exactly where
a third power lived? In our hours of play didn't we know

we inhabited a world where children live amazed
at the ignorance of adults? You and I and the lives we shed
like tadpoles on the way to legs, did we really lose these

to maturity? And where are the happinesses we dreamed
between hatchling and storm? In our flooded paddock
low-hanging branches were all we ever needed

to swing us above the deeps we mocked. So how
did we arrive at age's sober spot? Was it years of
weathering that stripped the aura from innocence?

You and I and the games we perfected, what now?
Is *true* only *true* if you perform a thing right?
We glow in the dark. We age further towards

youth. Perhaps we rooted so earthily, so deep,
so that now we can flower in a way that
balances the grief and joy of things.

Real Estate

CHERYL ADAM

The lawnmower towing the elderly lady had a mind of its own as it gathered speed down the sloping lawn. Luke watched her battle with the machine and then turned his attention back to the 'For Sale' sign on the property next door to hers.

All the renos had been done, and top dollar was expected these days in Melbourne. He sighed, knowing it would be too expensive for him. A spew of grass blew into his face. He coughed and rubbed his nose.

"Sorry!" the old girl called out. "It got away from me. I only mow downhill; haven't the breath to mow up the hill." She smiled, ready for a chat. Her head inclined towards the real estate sign. "Thinking of buying?"

"I'm looking, but I want something to renovate otherwise it's too pricey. Damn COVID has ruined everything." His eye followed the mowed strip up to her front door and noted the peeling paint and grass growing in the gutter. His brow lowered, thoughtful. She followed his gaze.

"Mine needs a lot of TLC." She took a step backwards, tugging at the lawnmower and slipped. Luke rushed forward, grabbing both her and the mower. Giving him a grateful smile, she straightened leaving him holding the bucking machine.

"It's a bugger to get up the hill."

"Let me finish the mowing for you." Her eyes widened.

"Well, that's kind of you. I won't refuse the offer, you know. Thank you." He gave his white knight grin. He would like to find out more about her. He guessed she was close to eighty.

"That deserves a big glass of my freshly squeezed orange juice and a piece of cake. My name is Jenny."

"I'm Luke. Nice to meet you, Jenny."

They sat in deck chairs on the porch looking at the clipped lawn, sipping orange juice. Luke wanted to see inside the house.

"Mind if I use your toilet?"

"Not at all, it's at the end of the hall on the right." He noticed the shoes lined up inside the door and undid his laces, pulling off his shoes to her nod of approval.

Inside the house it was still '60s original. He could knock out the wall between kitchen and dining room. Replace the kitchen. Having a separate toilet was good, but he'd upgrade the bathroom, move the laundry. Rip up the carpet and have polished floors throughout. There was a good size back yard with room for a pool. He hummed as he made his way back down the hall to the porch and Jenny.

"I noticed when I was mowing that the gutters need a clean. I could do that on the weekend if you like, it won't take long." The shine in her eyes hit his dart board.

"That is so kind of you, although …" she looked at her hands, embarrassed. "I'm on a pension and can't pay you much."

"I don't want money. I want to do a favour for a nice neighbour." He gave her a reassuring smile. "Do you have any children?" He saw her lips purse. "I'm sorry, I'm not trying to be nosey, just thought kids usually help their parents and there's a lot to be done around here so …"

"I have a married daughter in England. My partner died recently. She used to keep the repairs up but I'm not into DIY.

If you want to clean the gutters that would be appreciated, and I will make you a cake." Luke stood up to go.

"Deal. I'll bring my ladder next weekend."

The following weekend, the gutters cleaned, Luke sat on the porch with a cold beer and slice of apple cake. He listened to Jenny prattle while he planned his next job. The gate needed a new hinge.

A few months passed and Luke was now a regular on Jenny's porch, a 'bubble buddy' under the new COVID laws. Jenny had listened to his woes, the wife that had left him along with the proceeds from the sale of their house and how he had to live in a shoebox flat up the road, student accommodation, but the cheapest he could get.

"Are you looking at any more houses this weekend?" Jenny was interested in the real estate market, had been googling, hoping to find a house for Luke. His mouth turned down.

"It would be easier if businesses hadn't started collecting houses."

"I'll give you first option on mine if I decide to sell, but that's going to be a long time away."

"Might need to put that in writing," he said with a laugh.

She walked with Luke to the letterbox then put her hand on his arm.

"I forgot to ask if you would mind lending me your ladder? The man who fixed my television aerial said there's a bird's nest in the gutter and rain might cause a backup into the eaves. My ladder isn't long enough for me to reach though."

"Sure, I'll drop it off. I don't need it where I live. There's actually nowhere to store it at my place so you could keep it in your shed if you like?" He forgot to mention the dodgy rung. Jenny nodded; she had plenty of room. "Mind you don't climb up without someone there." His eyes crinkled. "Or you could wait until I can do it for you?" She shook her head. Heights didn't bother her. She'd been a climber in her youth, Mont Blanc her greatest achievement, the Blue Mountains her last. A ladder was a cinch.

The sprinkling rain reminded Jenny about the bird's nest. Donning her raincoat, she went out to the shed. Luke's ladder was heavy, one of the old wooden types. Dragging it to the house she realised she would need help to lift and prop it against the wall. She went down to her letterbox and waited for a passer-by. A kid on a bike stopped at her wave. Five dollars exchanged hands and the boy helped her erect the ladder.

Three bird's eggs were in the nest. A parent fluttered, frantic, in the overhanging gum tree. Jenny lifted the nest taking care not to disturb the eggs and carefully descended the ladder. She placed the nest beneath the tree in sight of the parent. Then she got underneath the ladder and pushed it back towards the tree, where it crashed against a sturdy branch. Jenny collected the nest, climbed up and wedged it amongst a tangle of new growth making sure the parent bird could see it. She was descending the ladder and only a few rungs from the ground when the dodgy rung gave way.

She flung her arm out to break her fall. Pain seared through her arm as she hit the ground. She heard the brakes of a car and a door slam before she fainted from pain.

Luke showed his fake COVID vaccination certificate to the busy receptionist who gave it a quick glance and directed him to Jenny's room. He entered and sat next to her bed. She smiled up at him.

"You won't be able to manage at home on your own so I was thinking I could sleep over?"

Jenny shook her head. No man had ever helped her dress let alone put her on the toilet.

"Thank you, Luke but the hospital has arranged a care programme for when I leave, and I've organised meals on wheels. But I like to do the crossword in *The Herald-Sun* and would be grateful if you could drop that in for me?"

Luke leant forward, elbows resting on his knees and tapped his fingers together. He had hoped she would jump at his offer.

"I'm just thinking, breaks take a long time to heal, especially when you're older, and the house might become a bit much for you. You might consider a nice retirement home. My mother loves hers." He shot her a look from under his brows. Jenny frowned.

"The only way I'll leave my house is in a box."

Luke didn't press the point; all he had wanted was to leave her with the thought.

Jenny was beaming from her couch, feet up in front of the tele, crossword finished on her lap when Luke walked in. The house sparkled from the efforts of the cleaner subsidised by the council. Had she known about the cleaning assistance she would have organised it a couple of years earlier.

"Make yourself a cuppa and come and join me or there's a beer in the fridge if you want."

Luke shook his head and plopped down next to her. He wasn't feeling well. The text message he had received last night said his results were positive. He didn't mention his COVID test to Jenny. He coughed and then covered his mouth. "A spot of asthma. Spring kills me." He picked up her crossword and pencil, scrutinised the page, and tapped the pencil against his lips. Gave another cough.

"Anything you're stuck on?" She pointed to six down. It was easy and she had saved it for him: Where had the Olympics originated?

"Greece," he said after a moment and wrote it down.

"My partner, Vivian, and I had planned to visit Greece but then she died," Jenny said, watching a bee settle on a blossom outside her window.

"Sell up and you can go." Luke's eyes shone down at her; red-rimmed from coughing. "I know someone who will buy it." She waved her strapped arm smiling gently.

"I'll have to get the arm fixed first."

Luke left Jenny's with hope in his heart and a cough that wracked his body.

The following day he woke with a throbbing head, body aching and a throat full of razor blades. He dragged himself out of bed, wheezing. He had to get *The Herald-Sun* for Jenny and check if she had COVID symptoms. It could be a death sentence at her age. Lucky he was only forty.

She met him at the door, eyes widening above her mask. "Goodness, you look awful. You need a doctor." She stepped back. "You had better not come in. I've had a positive COVID result and I'm in isolation." She sneezed, once, twice, three times. Luke glanced above her head at the pressed tin ceiling in the hallway. It was a feature he would keep.

"Here's your newspaper," he wheezed, thrusting it towards her.

"We've been in contact so you should get tested." Her eyebrows met. "You were coughing before me."

He looked away, unable to hold her gaze. "I have allergies, but I'll get tested." He was feeling dizzy and needed to get home and call a doctor.

The siren wailed. Luke lay on the gurney in the back of the ambulance, an oxygen mask covering his face, his breath rattling in his ears and a hammer pounding in his head. He had never felt so ill. He had a pang of guilt that Jenny would suffer like this.

Ten days later Jenny stood at the front desk reading a sign that said COVID PATIENTS ARE NOT ALLOWED VISITORS.

"Can I leave these for Luke Jones in ICU please?" The nurse nodded. She pulled the bunch of flowers and card out of her sling. Her broken arm had been her saviour. If it hadn't been for that, she might not have had her second vaccination and it would be her in the ICU and not Luke.

The gravity of his illness made Jenny consider her situation. COVID had changed the rules. She needed to visit her daughter in England and maybe do that trip to Greece for Vivian. Of course, it would have to wait until overseas travel was allowed. In the meantime, with the money she got from the sale of Viv's house next door she could renovate her place, sell, and cash in on the housing market. The renovations could be done while she was overseas. After that she could move to Brighton near her brother. She hoped Luke would recover although it wasn't looking good.

I don't post on Facebook

COLLEEN HIGGS

about the thirty witogies feasting on the honeysuckle bush
or how I'm thirty steps closer to getting divorced.

It's only three o'clock in the afternoon. And I'm tired.
The mediator isn't.

He says: she can have the house—that can be her pension.
I want her pension. It's not a house. I can't afford proper dentistry.
One by one I am losing my teeth, he says.

At last, we've reached an agreement. I am giving him my pension.

Blood from a stone.
I am the stone. There is no more blood.

After Dinner

ANGELA COSTI

I stand at my assigned gutter and watch for the lone car. Will there be one like last night, driving like a fretful canoeist about to plunge down the rapids? Tonight, the road is empty. I yell, *Remember, Remember, Remember* to the still air floating on this river of bitumen.

The neighbours living across the divide hear me, come out of their locked lives, wave their hands towards the voice filling the emptiness. I wave back. It's too dark for them to see my smile. A few more heartbeats and I turn my back to retrace my steps, down Gordon Street, across Lever Street, up Saunders Street, to number 46—my house known for its rundown fence, its greying pittosporum punching the power lines.

Even if I wanted to walk over the boundary road, I couldn't without the slap of fear. The Curse flies with the wind, swims with the water, feeds from the same plate. It's got them. Not us. The rules of lockdown divide us.

There are others like me. Middle-aged women. Leaving unscraped dishes in the sink, soiled soccer kits on the floor, addled fathers to pee in their pants. I count at least seven of us. We're growing by the night. Each of us wearing a silly animal, designs brave enough for sleep. Across my pyjama top, my lipstick poodle is cavorting with the night breeze, alive to the triggers of insomnia. There's a woman with purple and pink zebras, another with a penguin parading as Santa. We don't mingle. We keep to our regulated distances. One or two women give me a nod as if we're soldiers at the frontline.

These steadfast streets encircling my house, I dearly love with ambivalence, as a mother loves her children. Each house I pass offers its personality without discretion. Spilling their emotions like passionfruit tendrils as I walk past their open doors, naked windows, unstable gates. Never before have I come to know the intimate details of bedroom habits. The scenes and poses, a movie will edit, beg a gasp or a sigh from each of us. And there are those houses overwhelmed by screens zooming or avatars wrestling reality, where the bedtime story is survival of the games console. Shouts of rebellion and screams of anguish are no longer muffled during these months of reinventing the home.

As we pass Valencio's house, our backs stiffen. *Fuck, Bitch, Cunt*— stabbing blindly, accompanied with a smash. Us hoping it's not bone. He starts up before curfew ends. His wife, Katerina, is not in my group of nightwalkers. There's still time for her to join us. I can make out her silhouette in the hallway or is it the mop thrown into the coat rack? I'm always tempted to shout her name. Even though I've never met her, I know her well. I'm worried my calling will startle her fragile heart. I'm worried my calling will precipitate a conclusion she's not ready to live with. I wait a few minutes, hoping she will escape to the front verandah. But no, no. She hides in the deep folds of the house.

We resume our pace, a little slower, a little unsteady. Until we hear the song that makes our animals-of-thread jiggle, the way children instantly dance when they hear music they love, our steps align with the rhythm of the bass and didgeridoo, with the outpouring of endurance and survival. Danny's fanfare, courtesy of Yothu Yindi, singing about the continuing curse of two rivers separated for too long.

Danny's front yard is his home: the wood burner his stove, the eucalypts his fuel, the chairs and couches invitations to eat, sleep and watch these odd women with their walk to help them dream. Danny's large eyes invite one woman to step through his open gate and sit by the fire, watching it flare and subside along with the ups and downs of Danny's yarning.

After Danny's house is where most of us branch off. I continue to go straight, followed by one. Without the need for talk, we stop at Anita's house. She's in her front room. The lights blazing with her intensity. She's holding a stick in one hand, a paint can in another, she's crouching then standing, turning then plunging, the quick movements of a bird wishing to fly. Her canvas is always laid out like a rug, taking up most of her room. A few times, we've been lucky enough to see her creations. She walks them to her porch, their sweat and tears exposed, thankful for the fanning of night's air.

Sensing curfew has begun, I walk towards my house. No one behind me. All the women would have walked through their front gates by now. I walk through mine, open the fly screen and then the front door. There's no need for locks or keys.

Inside, the lights assault. The TV is protesting about protesters, showing streams of people walking the night, young, angry, scared. Mama is sitting on the couch, her hand of veins and bones holding her beloved gold cross, kissing it furtively. I take her hand as any mother would take a child's and walk her to her bedroom. Her special black dress for church is laid out on the bed, waiting to be worn. I help her get dressed, find her good shoes and handbag, make sure the chain holding her cross is not a threat to her neck. I leave her sitting on the bed with assurances I'll return in a few minutes, hoping she will stay.

I walk to the carport. The night is still teasing the wind. The back end of my car is covered with the toll of the year's seasons while the front wears the dust of disuse. There's only one corner that's kept clean. It's here that I find the matchbox with the finger-like matches to awaken the wicks of the hanging lamps. Their light animates the sombre faces of Christ and Mary. Illuminates Saint George, Saint Paraskevi and the others—stabbing a snake, levitating, communing with angels. Long ago, I expected a voice to emerge from this crowded corner of icons. Now I know their offering is silence.

Walking back into the house and to Mama's bedroom, I find her standing, wide-eyed and still, ready to be summoned. She follows me to that holy corner of the carport, facing east. Without fear or hesitation, Mama kisses each icon then sinks to the rug, turning her chest into a map of the cross with her right hand. Humble murmurings of gratitude rise and fall as she recounts the names of the living, beginning with her youngest grandchild, then her children, her siblings, her nephews and nieces, their children, her husband, and finally, herself.

Three Photographs

CARMEL MACDONALD GRAHAME

(i)
You might almost think of this as a black-and-white picture.
In fact, I am crossing a winter campus, tramping over snow,
freezing despite a padded coat and the hood hiding my face.
I could be listening to ELO—it was the Walkman decade—
and most likely to *Hold on Tight*, for its energetic yearning.
I could have been on my way that day to *Women's Studies—
A History of Motherhood*, where I had lately been discovering
the latter word was slanted, and relatively new to the lexicon.
Historians who made flat shoes attractive lectured in a theatre,
where what had been invisible was appearing. I was learning
to see myself differently, not to take womanhood for granted.

The days had a radical glitter, which struck me like frostbite.
Or it could also have been when I was studying the Romantics.
We memorised passages of Wordsworth, Coleridge, Blake …
and I would cross that icy, bone-cold, northern place reciting
lines from *The Prelude, Christabel, Songs of Innocence …*
Luscious poetry, at that stage of my life, was a dream infusion.
On mornings when the children were at school, I would read.
Most afternoons I worked in a local women's refuge.
The rest of time was spent home-making, making headway,
making love … for my sins, even making ballet tutus once,
always hoping to make a difference—look how young I was.

(ii)
Here, swansdown is like cirrus frozen in maternal fingers.
Tutus spring in petals of white net from ruched bodices.
I am in the company of pleasant women I no longer know,
stitching myself into a small girl's vision of becoming
a creature of the dance, lining it with feathers, abetting
her desire for flight; an aspiring Fonteyn, a willing mother.
She has said what she wants—that question madly echoing,
reducing us both to an *all* and still making my thoughts race
about forms of rigour, discipline, even tyranny and sacrifice.
This picture was taken when equality had just begun to mean
women being kitted out in camouflage-with-weaponry.

So, I imagine being there to dilate the feminine, laying claim
to art, beauty, grace, and, for our daughters' sake, peace.
I hear it: swansdown on straps too girls, lead mother instructs.
And, *Do you like it here?* The question always cornered me.
I would not have said that on the way my car slid on black ice,
so I drove into a snowdrift hoping to survive, cursing the place.
Or that when it came to tutus I was a mother out of her depth.
We would have firmly kept up a careful conversational rhythm,
trying for better than good enough, a conscientious collective
taking up needle and thread in the tradition of creative mothering—
see, my smile of surprise, and all of us almost choreographed.

(iii)
Afternoon light falls on a house like any other in the street,
except this one has been barred and bullet-proofed, discreetly.
Side fences, high and ordinary, keep sightlines to a minimum,
but I know a narrow path led to a security gate onto a backyard
called The Playground, with a swing, and camera surveillance.
You can see a wintry poplar spreads grey limbs above a path,
and patches of snow on squares of what, in spring, was grass.
Then, four wide steps lead to a door on a blunt front porch.

This red light was an intercom, the only way to gain access
to a house of last resort, where women brought their fear,
but only when they could bring the bewildered children too.

That day's life stories would have borne the usual bruises;
burns, incidents of servicing at gunpoint in kitchen, bedroom;
forced with axe or knife by a man whose hand-me-down rage
is personal, who might improvise or orchestrate his violence,
in any case saves it for home, blaming his ferocity on her face—
It's because I love you ... Now look what you've made me do ...
Leaving took courage, does still, since it goes on happening.
Inside, salvation-generosity spilled from a donations room.
The woman who ran the kitchen was a comfort food genius.
Define recovery, she would say if someone asked. *Takes time.*
Her father had killed her mother; she'd witnessed it, at six.

She sang along to Grace Jones—*sick and tired of this bullshit ...*
and the Annie Lennox mantra, *Sis-ters doin' it for themselves ...*
Downstairs, a child centre was more scrupulous than warm;
careful, no matter how professionally we cultivated kindness.
In a front office, social workers spoke of check-outs, intakes.
Counsellors dealt with fallout—medical, legal ... clients decided.
Volunteers did food shopping, child-minding, police escorts.
A filing cabinet contained the names of police never to be called,
trusted translators, donors and board members, and case-files
for court, for the women who did not, eventually, survive ...
Of course, none of this is visible, in the picture, from the road.

Where the Body is Buried

LUCY SUSSEX

It all started when Simo and I decided to treechange. Dead easy, people said; but what we got was a surprise, the dead in actuality. But I'm getting ahead of my tale. Let's start with a blank slate, what was left after the weed trees and scrub got cleared off our new country block.

The first day of the build, we learnt our site had human remains. We hit the freeway out of the city, to find on arrival a cop, crime scene tape and our new neighbours, stickybeaking. Downslope we saw excavations, the upturned loam, the bobcat halted before a hole. Within it was an unmistakable shape: a human skull.

How old was a question for the coronial workers, arriving in their van. They erected a tent, started digging. What they found next was a button, mother-of-pearl.

"Ancestor wear," said Simo, who does vintage.

No surprise in this locale. All around us stretched our new view: geology, old and newer, man-made. It mixed farm- and bushland, with the heaps and shafts of old goldfields. I might have majored in IT, but history had been a favourite uni subject. From that I knew those were wild and lawless times.

From Dr Alfred Cuthbertson, Meddlar's Creek goldfield, 1857

My dearest Mamma and Sisters,

July is Winter in the Antipodes, which will seem unusual to you in a Kent summer. We are not at a latitude nor altitude to have snow in July, odd though it may sound, but still experience frost and icy wind. Thankful I am that I abandoned gold-digging for medicine. Often I am paid in gold, dust and even tiny nuggets, which I will have made into brooches for all of you. The most popular here sport digger's spades and other implements, the size that only a dollhouse could use. Of course, you are beyond such playthings, except as adornment.

Let me describe my workdays to you. They begin with the sick congregating outside my slab and bark hut (so preferable to a leaky tent). Or I am called out to a half-dug shaft, containing a miner with a broken leg. And stranger summonses, like stories in a penny journal. Let me tell you of one …

We waited as the day progressed, bringing a forensic archeologist in a jeep. Dr Rani was visibly pregnant and very businesslike. As dusk fell, she gave us a gander, while the gurney got loaded into the coronial van. We saw anonymous bones, caked in dirt, and the remains of rotted garments. The skeletal hands were crossed over the chest.

"Laid out for a coffin?" I asked.

"Didn't get one," Dr Rani replied. "Just a shallow grave. But someone showed respect."

"Age?" Simo asked.

"Mid-1800s? There's two lots of shirt buttons, then more, larger, from a waistcoat and greatcoat. That rusty lump was a belt buckle, and see beneath the feet bones, hobnails. Got dressed for cold weather, wearing every bit of clothing possible, for warmth."

"How did he die?" Simo again.

A shrug. "No signs of violence. Yet."

So back we drove to the city, accompanied by unanswered questions.

From Alfred Cuthbertson, *continued, 1857*

One morning arrived a hulking, grizzled man, an Old Vandemonian for sure. His arms showed barbarous tattoos, and doubtless his back knew the lash. He summoned me to Magpie Gully, some distance away, where a poor miner needed my skills.

I hesitated, for rain loomed, but my supplicant offered gold. So, for the pity of it, and my womenfolk's brooches, I saddled my horse and accompanied him.

In the low ranges rising above the goldfield's flat are many gullies. Magpie we reached as the clouds opened, it being steep, rocky and supporting only two claims. One belonged to Bill, the only name he gave me. The other's name I never learnt.

I should explain that most men on the goldfields unite as 'mates' to share work and protect their claims from marauders. Others are solitary, called hatters. The Magpie miners had been hatters, keeping themselves to themselves. Only when the other had not worked for several days did Bill investigate.

Bill guided me to a meagre tent, within it a sad scene: little more inside than a stretcher-bed of sacking and gum saplings. Beneath a tattered blanket lay a figure white as wax, and almost as still. Here was a man so young he lacked the usual goldfields beard, emaciated under his layers of clothing. I touched his brow, hot with fever; heard his breathing.

Though I thought him unconscious, his eyes opened, and he drew up his hands in self-defence. I did not need to examine further to diagnose pneumonia. Nowhere was anything to eat, nor to steal.

"He needs nourishment," I told Bill. Also nursing, but where to find a Miss Nightingale on the rush? Even if the poor fellow could pay.

Bill said, "I can make gruel. And I watched my mother in the sickroom. I knows what needs to be done."

"God be thanked," I said, though from a Vandemonian I hardly expected tenderness.

And so I returned to my practice, to find some miners poisoned from eating possum pie, they claimed. In the days following I quite forgot Magpie Gully. Then arrived a boy astride a donkey.

"The Old Lag wants you," he said.

"Which one?" I said.

"At Magpie Gully. He paid me for this message and he will pay you too."

I saddled my horse again. The day was fine, but entering the gully it seemed the Valley of the Shadow of Death. I found my patient moribund but conscious. The tattered blanket lay underneath him now, a coverlet of possum-skins, crudely cured and sewn, retaining what warmth was left to him. Bill smoothed the dying pillow, stuffed with raw wool. I saw a bowl by the bed, its gruel barely touched.

The dying miner spoke despite the death rattle, his voice a husky whisper: "I give thanks to my benefactor."

"He has served you well?" I asked.

"Aye, but I was badly served afore, by want and cold. They have done their worst.

Doctor, I beseech you, take this letter from my hands and send it Home."

It was sealed, and directed to a name not uncommon, the address being in the Scots borders.

"Soon I will be gone. I want no disturbance. When I have breathed my last, bury me just as I am, with no shroud but my old blanket. Dig a grave and lay me down, without parson, or prayer, and heap the good earth over my remains."

I nodded, since I have found it is best not to contradict any last wishes—it distresses the dying.

Bill followed me outside the tent, with my fee.

"Sir, I'll watch for the last breath."

"You are," I replied, "a natural gentlemen."

"You would not a said that in old Hobart town, where I did my time for robbery with violence."

I shook his hand, dirty and rough with toil though it was.

He came closer, displaying jagged, yellow teeth, and murmured: "I do believe the poor soul be not one of us, sir. But I won't find out for sure."

"What do you mean?" I said, my mind full of nameless fears.

He said, "I think that hatter be no man …"

Several days later Dr Rani rang with the news, to our amazement.

"That body's a woman?"

"No doubt about it," she said through the speakerphone.

"But wearing men's clothes, on a goldfield?" Simo said.

On the television, muted when Dr Rani rang, the news reported yet another woman murdered this year.

"Not a fashion statement. Safer that way," I said.

"If against the law and the Bible then," said Dr Rani.

"She wasn't the only one," I said to Simo.

After Rani rang off we hit the internet, journeying through the history of women in men's guise from soldier gals to novelists walking the Parisian streets. The most famous Australian example was Edward de Lacy Evans, wearing the pants for thirty years and two marriages, both to women. Lived in Daylesford, small wonder.

From Dr Alfred Cuthbertson, *continued, 1857*

Just then we heard the laboured breathing cease. We entered a silent tent, to find my patient departed from this life. I felt for the lost pulse, then crossed the wan hands over the breast. Bill it was who reached out and closed those unseeing eyes, as gentle as a butterfly.

"And now," he said, "we do as was wanted. God knows all secrets, and His mystery is not for us."

"Amen," I said.

We removed Bill's borrowed bedding, and folded the blanket over the dead. Bill took one end and I another, and we carried what was no burden to the edge of the claim. There, in ground the poor miner had disturbed already fruitlessly, we dug a grave, using Bill's shovels. Shallow it was but still deep enough to deter those carrion-eaters, the dingo or native dog. The dead—I will not nor cannot write man, nor woman—we laid to rest, then covered over with a final blanket of dirt and stones.

I posted that letter the next day.

Dearest Mother, you may think my tale indelicate, but do not judge the poor fellow, even if fellow be he none. More important is the story of a truly Christian kindness, as is beloved by the Supreme Being.

I know your habit is to read my letter first, then to the dear girls. If you believe the matter unsuitable for my sisters, then you may burn it.

Your loving son, Alfred.

Our build went ahead, without further discoveries. The coroner's court determined: person unknown, cause of death unknown. Who was she? We trawled through Trove, visited the historical society, even consulted the Goth couple who ran ghost tours at the old regional asylum. No answer came at all. We had found a mysterious lady and that was the way she would remain.

"What happens to the bones?" asked Simo.

My feeling also. We drove around the country churchyards, saw the neglect, the vandalised graves. Whoever she might be, we felt a responsibility for wherever she might rest. The build progressed, our home nearing completion. No way we could return her under our floorboards, but nearby?

We hired a landscaper specialising in native plants, and then sounded out the local sculptors. Then we made submissions to the authorities. Finally, on a fine day, we held a gathering, part house-warming, part homecoming.

Everybody who had come to care got an invitation: friends, the new neighbours, historians, a regional journalist, the builders and Dr Rani, who brought her baby. A bush band performed a goldfields song, then the Ladies in White lowered an eco-coffin into a little fenced space, where our garden met remnant bush. Overlooking it was a small statue we had commissioned, part angel, part abstract. It bore no name, as seemed fitting for an anomymous lady. We laid the dead to rest again, we hoped in peace.

After everyone had left, Simo and I sat by the grave with a bottle of prosecco and our best glasses. We were two women dressed like men, Simo dapper in her vintage, me an IT scruff, but that was legal now. The setting sun shone on our wedding rings, something else permitted, and we drank a toast to whoever she was.

As it was a slow news day, the journo's story went viral. Other press came calling, even the television stations. You can see us all via ABC-iview, *Australian Story*, with the epilogue: a sprightly old lady called Elfrieda visiting, carrying an archive box. She opened it to show pages of scribbly Victorian handwriting.

Elf said: "I have something for you, a letter from my many-times-great-uncle Alfred."

And so we got, if not the full story, then as much as we were ever likely to know.

Souvenirs

CAROL LEFEVRE

Hot nights, when it's impossible to sleep, Lily hears voices in the whirr of the fan. She gropes in panic for the light switch, or bolts upright in the dark to listen. An intruder could break in without her knowing, could sleep in one of the unused beds and creep away next morning. But it's never an intruder, only the fan voices. Sometimes they sing, other times they squabble and scream; she strains for meaning but cannot identify words, or even a language. Occasionally the voices sound like children, and those are by far the worst.

When Dahlia her home help arrives, Lily asks her to open the sash window in the dressing-room—when this window is raised it hoists a fly-screen out of the wall cavity. It reminds Lily of a house where she and Tom once lived. Most of its windows had been painted shut, and when they freed them, they had been thrilled to discover the old-fashioned fly-screens. The sofa in the dressing-room is where she reads before she goes to bed, or in the early mornings. For one thing there are no mirrors, and for another she sometimes sees Tom there, even though he's never lived in this Adelaide settler's cottage. Lily sees him pulling on a shirt in front of the open wardrobe, or rifling through the drawer that, in her mind, is where he would have kept his socks. These sightings only occur in the dressing-room, but they console Lily when she wakes in the dark at some small noise. Oh, it's only Tom, she thinks, looking for something in the wardrobe.

Lily sometimes sleeps on the sofa, where the night air falling through the fly-screen rolls over her in cooling waves. All those years they spent on that island in the Irish Sea, where it was never anything but cool; those ferry crossings, the sky like an army blanket suspended above them, blocking out the real sky, which for most of Lily's life had only ever been the bluest blue. On the ferry, when the island suddenly rose up out of the lead-grey sea, how her spirits would plummet to be returning to a place that would never be home.

At first, she had tried to love it, even with its dearth of trees. The beam of a lighthouse had passed over the front windows of their house, a symbol of safety but also of peril. And when the foghorn sounded its desolate cry, it was as if she had laid out the tarot cards and turned up Death, or the Nine of Swords. Why not The Sun, or The Lovers, or even The Fool? She could have coped with those cards.

Dahlia and her husband are to celebrate their wedding anniversary with a cruise. They'll sail from Sydney, visiting New Caledonia and other Pacific islands.

"What will I bring you as a souvenir?" she says.

Lily shakes her head. "Oh no, Dahlia, I don't need anything."

Souvenirs can't be bought for other people, she thinks. You choose a souvenir as you choose a memory to keep from among the millions of moments that will slip into the unremembered past. Looking at Dahlia's good-natured face, Lily ponders the strangeness of her offer, but after all, it will be the first time Dahlia has left Australia.

"I'll surprise you then," she says.

Lily asks Dahlia if she plays cards. "It could be useful," she says, "Something to pass the time between islands."

At her next visit Dahlia brings a pack of cards, and Lily shows her how to play Babu. Tom's parents had learned the game during a year in St Lucia, and when Lily and Tom had visited them there, they had sat over cards night after night on the terrace, mosquitos biting, and moths the size of small birds flapping around the outside lights. Her in-laws had been competitive; they became disgruntled when they lost. In St Lucia, Lily had gradually needed more and more rum punch to endure those card sessions.

"There are five rounds, and each round has a different objective," she explains to Dahlia.

They sit at the kitchen table to practise, and Dahlia asks if it's all right to take off her shoes. "This ingrown toenail is killing."

Lily shrugs; she is wearing slippers. "In the first round, the aim is to take no tricks." She deals the cards and shows Dahlia how to win by losing. "The object of the second round is to have no hearts left in your hand when the first person goes out."

It is the same for the next round with no queens, and in the fourth round the player caught holding the king of hearts pays a hefty penalty. The final round, jacks, ends up laid out like a game of patience. Dahlia nods; her husband plays patience on the computer.

"Then it all starts over, until you're sick of it. The lowest scorer is the winner."

With Gina they'd played a card game at the kitchen table, a game Lily's father had taught her when she was young. She pictures the fan of cards in Gina's hands, her dear face puckered in concentration.

Playing Babu after all these years, that final round with the lines of cards, each suit descending in order from its jack, has reminded Lily unpleasantly of the barn dance she and Tom went to up by the village church—a *ceilidh*. She had still been trying to love the island then, telling herself she would become accustomed to its treeless contours, and to the claustrophobia whenever the weather closed in. Gina had been due to start school the following September, and they had been about to put her name down at the small school in the village.

The farmer whose land adjoined their house was at the barn dance with his wife, a young woman with ginger hair and a reticent, white bun face—Lily knew her from play group. Lily had never spoken to the farmer, but she and Tom often saw him on his tractor, rattling over the fields close by the house, and they would wave to him, and he'd wave back in a friendly manner. But at the dance, when he'd had a bit to drink, the farmer had cornered Lily and demanded to know where she was from, even though the whole village knew she was Australian.

"What passport've ye got?" A young, wiry man with pale, straggly hair and colourless eyes, he'd stood facing her with his feet apart, swaying slightly, his drink-flushed face belligerent.

Tom's passport was English. Hers was Australian. And Gina— Lord, Gina's was complicated! Because she'd been born far from either of them, in Chile, though in the Australian court, when her adoption was finalised, the judge had said gravely that from then on it would be as if Gina had been born to them, their own child. Gina had eventually disabused them of this, forcing Lily and Tom to see that it had never been possible, never been true. But on the night of the dance, that grief was still far off.

Lily had told the farmer she held an Australian passport.

His face had twisted with rage. "An why're ye here then, livin' on land that belonged to my great-grandfather, and his father?"

Lily still felt fiercely that the red dirt of Australia was in her bones; there was nowhere she belonged more. Not in the way Indigenous people belonged, she acknowledged that. But then, being white, she had roots that stretched back to what one of her uncles still referred to as 'the Old Country', and there she was in a corner of that ancestral soil with a farmer drunkenly shouting that she should clear the fuck off his land.

The farmer's wife had appeared beside him, blotchy with embarrassment.

"Take no notice," she said, "he's got the drink on him." She leaned towards Lily, placatory. "We're friends, aren't we? Our kids play together?"

But Lily had known then that they would never be friends, however long they knew each other. She and Tom and Gina would always be strangers. At school, among their offspring, and the offspring of other locals, Gina's looks would mark her out as different; she might even be bullied. Next morning, while the farmer was likely sleeping off his hangover, Lily had made enquiries about enrolling Gina at a private school at the far end of the island where at least there were other non-local children.

Lily and Dahlia play a last round of Babu, and Dahlia is the first to go out.

"Well, I'd better finish up," she says, a winner's grin lighting her face.

While Dahlia pushes a mop over the kitchen floor Lily stares at the cards, still divided into four long rows, with no mixing of hearts, diamonds, clubs, and spades. Yes, that's why this game always brings up that awful night, and the hatred she had seen in the farmer's eyes because they were not his kind, not fit to line up with them, let alone live on what had once been their land.

Lily has few souvenirs of her time on the island—a pewter brooch in the shape of a mythical creature, the *cabbyl-ushtey*, or Manx water horse, a cruel and destructive creature said to inhabit ponds and streams. It is a striking piece, but when she'd bought it she hadn't understood its nature. She will ask Dahlia if she'd like it, and if not she'll put it in the bag she's filling for the charity shop. Then there is a handwoven blanket, and from the comforting distance of Australia Lily can admire its bog and peat-coloured wools, the soft hues of mountain heather that fleck the tweed.

The object that causes her the greatest heartache is a small white china thimble with a picture on it of the island's Laxey Wheel. It was acquired on one of those ferry crossings, the start of a summer holiday in Scotland. Gina had wandered off to the ferry's souvenir shop alone and returned clutching the thimble. She had used her holiday money to buy it for Lily.

In those days Lily had sewed to distract herself—cross-stitch samplers, patchwork quilts, stabbing at them with various needles. Her favourite thimble had belonged to her grandmother; it was silver, and fitted perfectly. The china thimble was clunky and uncomfortable, and with a picture on it that in Lily's opinion was ugly.

"Oh! You shouldn't have spent all your pocket money on this," she'd scolded.

Gina's face, expectant and full of suppressed pleasure, had frozen, and then turned blank. Lily could have cut out her own tongue. Hastily, she had promised that she would use the thimble, she had thanked Gina, and kissed her, but all these years later the memory is still like a knife-twist in Lily's heart. The china thimble sits on the dresser in her bedroom. Though ugly, she can never dispose of it, for the thimble contains the dregs of whatever childhood happiness had been Gina's, before it had slithered away into the great dark pool of the unremembered.

Dahlia's head appears around the door—fizzing dark hair, eyes bright with excitement. Tomorrow she and her husband fly to Sydney to begin their cruise.

"I wrote down the rules," she says. "No tricks, no hearts, no queens, no king of hearts, and last is jacks?

"Perfect!"

Dahlia closes the front door, and as silence settles over the rooms Lily longs to speak to Tom. For who else could understand the latent threat of cards lined up underneath the jacks, or that the story of their lives has somehow become encrypted in the rules of a card game? Only Tom understands the depth of grief that resides in the china thimble. In the dressing-room Lily waits, her eyes fixed on the sock drawer.

Playing Dolphins

MARY GOSLETT

She has reached the suburbs of her childhood and adolescence. Her father still lives around here somewhere. She pulls to the side of the road, exhausted. In the distance is the Catholic school she attended for so many bleak years. Nothing has changed. Shabby, lazy buildings. Tired people.

Shocked at the strength of her anger, she drives closer to the church and sits in the car park. Can hear the thin sound of chanting children's voices from a nearby classroom. Pictures a child sitting just as she had sat; desperately wanting to know what is sinful about her because knowing would make it possible to atone. Be forgiven. Loved.

She drives further west, horrified at housing tracts where once had been scrub and bush. Mile after mile of blonde brick houses cram against each other. Scorched lawns have replaced tea tree and turpentine. Black and ochre swathes of the latest back-burn have succeeded only in encouraging thick re-growth.

There is so much suburban development she gets lost. The old poultry farm is gone, and houses stand where feral gooseberry bushes and lantana had been thickest. There is a padlocked barrier across the private access road, and she can't drive any further. Not really believing she's doing it, she locks the car, climbs the gate and starts down the hill.

Once out of the blank stare of the houses her body responds to the bush. It's a very steep, rutted road, clinging to the side of the hill. It falls away sharply to the left where she knows there is a creek that swells with rain. Thick, close vegetation. Gymea lilies, ferns, tough bracken, mosses. The pull on her calves as it gets steeper is very familiar. They used to have to walk up the hill to get eggs from the poultry farm, and her body still knows how to lean in going uphill, lean back to balance going down.

She'd forgotten the beauty. Can feel herself settling. Her mind is calming as her nose takes in the tang of eucalypt and musk of earth. Feels like she could eat the rich dark loam, grab handfuls and crunch and lick. She gasps when she catches sight of the ancient grandmother Angophora that has always stood at the only flat section of the road. A majestic, gnarled trunk with deep, thick, red sap seeping from just underneath a large burl. She strokes it. Nothing ever felt so smooth and alive as this.

She remembers.

Remembering brings her back, and her stomach knots. She strides on downhill, brushing childhood bushes; egg and bacon flowers, spider bush. She hears a rustle in the undergrowth and sees them again—she and her little sisters throwing bantam eggs at a goanna. Leftover, too-small eggs they had been given at the poultry farm. She and her sisters, ready to pass on the rage.

From the bottom of the road she can see down to the river. She had loved that river. Knew its smells; its moods; the way it silvered; which winds caused it to turn grey.

She keeps walking, sees the carport the Father had built. Endless months of his rage as he tried to get the measurements right and fought to get it level on the steep slope. Trembling, she walks to the back of the structure, reaches out, leans on a beam and looks down towards the river.

She looks around again to make sure she's in the right place.

The house is gone.

She's disoriented, bewildered. Where is the pencil pine that used to grow just there? Where is the mulberry tree that the Father would make them climb to pick the berries for his favourite dessert? After long hot days at school, they would be made to pick his berries before allowed to swim.

She makes her way down further, navigating broken steps and sunken cement. At last she can recognise something: the cracked and broken tiles of the bathroom floor. She is shaken, dazed, flooded with images.

The difficulty growing up in that house had not just been the atrocities they were subjected to. It was that the children all believed they *were* the nasty, deceitful little mongrels they were told they were, and that the floggings were necessary to beat out the evil and make room for possible salvation.

The silence of others also seemed to reinforce that the punishments were both necessary and deserved. In the bath at the age of five, a family friend remarked on the bruises on her buttocks, and the Mother laughed and said you know what she's like, always falling over. She could see the friend's willingness to accept the story, and her acceptance made it truth. No one asked why her brother winced when he moved, why they all flinched when the Father made a sudden movement.

With the house gone, there is no evidence. She can't point to the hole in the wall, saying that happened when the Mother tried to hit her with the vacuum cleaner, or tell of the belting given when she missed. Can't show the corner where the Father made them bend over while he beat them with his belt or show the stairs where she crouched listening to siblings get punished and praying she wouldn't be next.

She had longed to escape; dreams were full of flying. During the day she'd practice by running down the straightest stretch of steps beside the house. The section was broad and shallow, and she could get up real speed. She would run faster and faster, leaping two at a time, run and run. But she'd always fall, never gain uplift. Knees and shins and palms were covered in scabs. In her dreams she'd fly down over those same steps, skimming and not falling. Then she'd be in the kitchen, flying in circles above the table and over their heads, uncatchable. Over the heads of honorary aunts who never earned their title. Never took her away.

Violence was always unpredictable, but somehow dusk invariably brought yet more slaps, tears, yells. All of the kids were most likely to slip-up then. Forget what had been hidden, confuse lies and truth, get beaten for honesty because fear made them forget what version had already been told in a desperate bid to escape a belting. Dusk was despair. The currawong's call echoed their loneliness.

Dusk also signalled night, which was even worse. Nights praying he wouldn't come to their rooms, into their beds.

She continues down the broken steps to the overgrown lawn and then to the river. The wharf the Father had built was still there. Ugly cement cinder blocks, no child's footprint immortalised on the path. A monolith. They'd carried heavy buckets of wet sand, two at a time to keep them balanced. At fourteen she'd had the biceps of a brickie.

It's low tide and she can see the small rocks and pebbles that litter the dark grey river sand. The Father had hated those pebbles and stones and made them pick them up each day. He also made them rip out the river weed; both tasks as never-ending as his need for control.

To the right is the spot where the neighbours tipped their over-full toilet pans at night thinking that no one would notice the turds caught in that same seaweed the next day. Having to take messages next door was terrifying, her fear of their dog loosening her bowels. It would slink up behind her, nipping and biting at her heels.

The water is cool on her feet. The ooze between her toes enveloping, sensual. A cloud drifts over the sun. On grey days they used to wander along and lift rocks in the mud and search out crabs. Small grey-brown creatures they were expert at catching. The crabs were roughly square, with soft pale legs and eyes on stalks. She and her sisters would put them in plastic ice cream containers, with some sand and small stones, maybe some strands of the slimy seaweed. Sometimes they would check them the next day, sometimes not for several days. There would only ever be one left. The biggest one. Maybe just some legs or shells of the others that had been eaten.

The kids had been like these crabs, turning on each other because they couldn't escape.

She eases into the water and floats, remembering how the river had always held her. She had never been afraid of it, not even when there were king tides that made the water a deeper green than ever before.

She sees her girl-child self, long-legged and skinny, standing at the riverbank with wary eyes and clenched fists. A sob forces itself out and, moaning, she reaches out to the child, clasps the fragile fingers.

Together they dive and splash, playing the old game of dolphins, an unending series of dives that leaves her dizzy and gasping. She breaks her own record of thirteen underwater somersaults in one breath. The girl-child is laughing, applauding, cheering.

They shiver and giggle as they lie recovering on the wharf's hot cement. As she dresses again, the girl-child slips in with her. She's glad she wore baggy clothes now.

About Geese

SUNITI NAMJOSHI

The golden goose got so tired of people filching her eggs, hanging about and trying to persuade her to lay half a dozen eggs all at one go and then asking whether she could possibly do some platinum ones that she decided to ask a wise old goose what she could do to stop all this nonsense.

The old goose didn't even pause to think before she honked, "Either stop laying eggs or glut the market." The golden goose didn't argue—nobody argues with wise old geese—but she went away sighing. She liked laying eggs, but not so many and not so often as to glut the market.

Meanwhile the petitions and the pilfering and the attempts at persuasion went on and on. The goose turned to her cousin, who was inclined to be bossy, but was generally considered extremely practical. "Cut your costs and increase your profits. And make your eggs smaller," she told the golden goose. The goose thanked her and went away sighing. She didn't like producing sub-standard eggs.

A few days later when she woke from a nap, she found a strange-looking goose staring at her. "Please go away," the golden goose begged. "I don't want good advice. And I'm not going to make my eggs any larger or smaller."

"Oh I haven't come about your eggs. I am a poet and you are a legend. I wanted to write a story about you," the bedraggled goose replied.

"Oh, all right," the golden goose murmured and fell asleep again. When she woke up, the poet goose was still there.

"Have you written your story?" she asked politely.

"Yes," replied the bedraggled one. "It goes like this. There was once a goose who laid golden eggs. This was quite an achievement, but she got fed up with people going on and on and on about her eggs so she hired a publicist to persuade everyone that her eggs were worthless. The publicist succeeded, and the goose had her fill of peace and quiet. But then she started missing the fuss and the frenzy, so she asked the publicist to persuade everyone that her eggs were priceless. The publicist succeeded and so on and so forth." The poet goose stopped.

The golden goose stared. At last she said, "Well, I take your point. Thanks."

And so the poet goose waved and went on her way feeling extremely pleased with herself.

The Cry

RENATE KLEIN

I haven't spoken about this for a very long time.

I couldn't.

Of course, the Big Master died—he had to, because every cell of my being willed itself to withdraw my energy.

And it worked. He was dead and I was alive.

But I was bruised and battered, a shadow of my former self.

There was the obvious physiological degeneration. I virtually had to rebuild both chambers, connecting tissue, filaments. Oh, and the big muscle had suffered greatly. That took ages to heal. Still hasn't completely, but I cope.

I was broken and I kept asking myself again and again how is it possible that we live in a world where such atrocities are allowed to happen?

How did it come to this? Why is no one crying out, shouting from the rooftops, "Stop this barbarism, stop it once and for all!"

But there was only silence and in my darkest moments I had visions of millions of others like us: used and abused, tortured, and often killed.

And then there was the grief. Deep, miserable, despondent grief. Ongoing. I still can't cope with it.

I tried to gain distance and travelled. I lay in Italian meadows and smelt English roses. I became drowsy from the heavenly scent of the blue lotus flowers in India.

I grew stronger; my blood came back.

And then, after a long time of trying to avoid my fate, I forced myself to be courageous. I knew I needed to go back. I couldn't just put my head in the sand forever. (How funny, as if I had a head.)

And yet I hesitated, like I was paralysed. Immobilised with grief. Some days, all I could do was cry.

The moment arrived when I knew now was the time to go back. But before I returned to where I had come from, I decided I had to be brave and face my fear straight on.

So, I went back to the place where the crime had taken place. And I felt it happening all over again.

The dread.

The anguish.

The pain.

The cut.

And the cries, not just mine.

The odiousness of the body into which I was plunged. The smells—disgusting.

More pain, more cuts.

And then the sewing up. I panicked. I could not move. I cried. Oh, did I cry.

But I also remembered the great wave of energy when my resistance began. When I decided once and for all that he had to die. Even if I died with him.

But I didn't. I am still alive.

As I approached the place where I had come from, all the familiar smells were in the air. So sweet, so pungent. They got stronger and stronger. My siblings, my friends. Everyone—but not her. Not ever again.

Soon after they had spotted me, I was encircled and kissed and nuzzled. It was so sweet. I tried not to swell up too much with love. I am not well enough to do that. But it felt good to be home.

"We missed you so much."

"We were so worried."

"We did not know what had happened to you."

"Where did you go?"

I tried to answer their questions, but I felt myself tire … and my unbearable sadness started to come to the surface again.

But they wouldn't let up.

"Do you know you are very famous?"

"Do you know they framed your poem?"

"Do you know it led to a worldwide revolt? An epiphany really. This crime is never ever going to be repeated. Country after country abolished it. You must be so proud of yourself."

I listened to their outpourings until they brought me my poem, framed with glistening stones—like teardrops. Or maybe just tears.

"You also won many prizes and they paid you a lot of money."

"Money," I said. "And what did you do with this money?"

This seemed to be a difficult question to respond to, but after some silence, one brave voice answered me.

"We invested it in … in the truffle bank, so that now every Monday, we get a delivery of the finest truffles in the land. And this will go on forever and ever. We will bring you some, they are delicious."

I tried to smile, but the pain was getting so much worse. I must not be as well-healed as I thought.

"We also did something else, but we're not sure how to tell you."

"Just say it. I will cope."

"We bought a beautiful pink plaque for … her grave. We thought you would like that if you ever came back."

I tried to show my appreciation, but I was racked with so much pain and grief, I was barely able to continue.

"Where is it? Show me the way. I want to go there by myself."

And so, it came that I visited the grave which has a beautiful pink plaque that simply says, "The evil must stop."

I had brought the framed poem and as I lowered it onto the soil, the teardrops became real tears and mixed with the red ones from me.

I had always known she would not survive. You can't live when your heart gets ripped out. Taken, not given. For an unworthy tyrant.

I said, "I'll read you the poem that brought so much change. No pig will die any more, they can all live in peace."

Once upon a time there was a
blue frog
and a yellow cow
and a red red dog
but what about the pink pig?

"The Big Master needs a new heart," the doctors decreed, "and the pink pig is the one we'll get it from."

"Why me?" cried the pig, "my heart is pink and happy and loving—all qualities the Big Master will not want at all."

"No matter," said the doctors, "we have decided. Your heart it is."

No screaming or pleading, no tears, no whimpering helped—
the pink pig was strapped to the operating table and, with a
syringe stuck in her hind leg, she passed out. Then the knife
plunged in and revealed the very pink, very alive, very rapidly
beating heart.

"A beautiful heart," the doctors said, "it will suit the Big Master;
it will make him well."

But when they proceeded to peel free the heart muscle,
to loosen the filaments and sever the blood vessels, the pig—
or was it her heart?—began to speak quite unexpectedly.

"I will," it said, "not obey the Big Master for he is not the
Master of the Heart."

"I will," it said, "shrivel and turn yellow and putrid, as is the
Master's flesh."

"I will, above all, cry."

Once upon a time there was a
blue frog
and a yellow cow
and a red red dog

and now you know what happened to the pink pig.
And her heart.
Or do you?

And so, it came that the poem's words draped themselves over
the grave and the plaque and left just a little space for me to lie
down next to her.

"Peace at long last," I whispered, "for both of us. We are
together again."

And with these words, I just slipped away. I guess it was the
only homecoming possible.

Birds

JORDIE ALBISTON

& there are sixty-eight trees & a flock
of fourteen no sixteen corellas &
me the only one black   how I want to
won't turn back   how whiteness intrudes   how white-
ness ever excludes   there are too many

places here without you   the too empty
spaces the sun on the run the too sky
full of itself   I sob against dashboard
no no more   my tears the most rain here for
years   & the cattle trucks pass   each smelling

of terror   & I pray die well though they're
already dead   there are sixty-eight trees
only one corella   the rest have gone
& like me she should be at home   it is
night-time now   the dandelion has blown

Lost Bird

MERLINDA BOBIS

She's feared. She's fearless. How the writers speak of her, especially the first-book novelists. Always, their wish and dread that she'd review them. Oh, to have her nod of approval, maybe that rare praise. Even only a crumb, so you have to excavate the text to find it. "Fearless and brilliantly written," some grudgingly say about her incisive renditions of insight after insight as she takes on a novel, any novel. As if she wrote it herself and had known all the writers' manoeuvres all along, especially their missteps. As if she had looked into their hearts. And found them wanting. She's the toughest critic this side of town.

"And that happy ending, hah!"

"Isn't that what we all hope for?"

"Is it?"

"Hope. Why we write."

"It's sentimental, plus all that unbridled grief."

"So, it's not credible?"

"I didn't write that —"

"You suggest it in your final paragraph. You equate credibility with emotional rendition."

"I was quite kind, considering it's soppy."

"Ever the authority on emotion."

"I did a PhD on affect —"

"Is it about you or the book?"

"Are you with me or against me?"

"You plucked out all the birds from her sky."

"What did you say?"

Poet dares not repeat what she just whispered about Critic's review of a novel some months ago. Besides, tonight's especial. They've just caught up again after half a year of silence. Oh, their on-and-off friendship. Because they always argue. Then have a falling out. Then reconcile. How many times now? So, just shut it. Remember, you asked her to be your date tonight. To make up. Again. It's reality. Sisterhood doesn't happen because of like sex. Sisterhood has to be negotiated. And we learn how, we learn, or try to.

Poet and Critic, friends since school days, toast with champagnes before sitting down for the awarding. The room begins to hush as the house lights dim and the emcee takes her place at the podium.

Critic squeezes Poet's hand. Clammy. "I hope you win."

Poet squeezes back, whispers, "Thanks." It's good to have her friend here to grace this special night. She understands *this*, supports it, even if she was bristling earlier, well, as always when she's crossed. Poet smooths her pants, feels the electricity of silk and the moment. She didn't expect to be shortlisted for this award, but now that she's here, well, she hopes to win. Critic knows hope too, how to dash it—oh, c'mon, you're friends again … wonder if she read my book, wonder what she thought of the bird poems … Through the emcee's welcome, Poet hears a fluttering.

Early morning in bed and she picks up the book again. She won, good on her. I'm glad I don't do poetry, doesn't give enough room to manoeuvre. Aw, do be happy for her. Critic can't sleep, despite the three nips of whiskey since she got home, after all those champagnes at the awarding. She went to bed still in her "nice frock," so her friend said, hugging her. Tightly. She hugged back, as tightly. "I frocked up for you," she wanted to say but bit her tongue. She strokes the book cover: robin roosting on palm. Ugh, sentimental! Aw, do be kind. She gets up, opens the window. The sky is darker tonight. Ah, her poems, her birds. *Her birds.*

They were fourteen then. Had been in school together from age ten or thereabouts. Two very different peas in a pod, a teacher said. *That* teacher. Called her friend "a nice, well-behaved kid" and her, "the little brat." They were neighbours, so they walked to school together, then home, but not straight home. They explored the side streets, then the bit of bush up that small hill. *Their* hill. How they loved the birds. They watched. Together. They listened. Together. They whistled the birdsongs. Together. And they played a game each time: writing words into the birdsongs. Until they turned fourteen.

Memory's a burden, forgetting even more so. Critic closes the window, pours herself more than a nip. She won't be able to do any work tomorrow, no, it's bloody today now! Who said whiskey helps, but she downs it anyway then slumps on the bed, wide awake at 4 a.m.

"So, what did you think." It isn't a question now.

Poet's fishing, Critic thinks. She didn't respond to her two text messages asking *the question* after her win. *What did you think of my book?* Even an award-winner still seeks her approval. But she doesn't do poetry. So, she didn't respond.

"Did you read it?"

Over the phone, the anxiety is acute.

"No time, too many deadlines, sorry."

"I see, don't bother."

"Of course, I'll read it later." She read it on that sleepless night after the win. She was impressed but doesn't want to say. "So, how are things with you?"

"So-so. And with you?" Poet asks in return.

"Well, like you, the usual."

She inquires about her, she does the same. She hugs, she hugs back.

"Would you like to go for a drink sometime?" Critic tries to make up.

No response.

"You still there?"

She's hung up.

Silence returned with silence.

She thinks about her now as she reads the rejection slip, then tears it up. Third rejection, third tearing. But Critic consoles herself. This isn't her genre, it's just play. Besides, *this* bloody slip is probably payback from the journal's editor, because of 'a cool review' that she did of his latest novel, and he's a big fish too. But she was fair. His book didn't really hang together like his earlier ones, which she'd praised. On the desk, the torn bits make her think of her friend before she won her award, no, before she started publishing books, when she was just beginning to submit poems to journals. She used to call her then and do a big weep after each slip like this. Not me, Critic shrugged, scooping the bits to the waste bin. She's made sure it was torn into unreadable bits and disposed of. Her little secret: she started writing poetry last year, well, just a break from novels, from reviewing them. She doesn't do poetry, really.

The whiskey burns her throat as she re-reads her poem that the journal turned down. Third time unlucky. Oh, well, she's not *The Poet*, certainly not then.

They were fourteen, neighbours, schoolmates, besties forever. And they loved words. From writing words into birdsongs, they moved on to writing ditties, rhyming stuff. She'd write a line, she'd write the next, she'd write another, she'd pick it up from there, and so on. Wordplay. They never really called it *poem*. Until that summer when her friend began writing 'her own stuff' (like a poem, y'know), urging her to do the same. And she'd dedicate it to her, recite it to her as they walked home arm in arm. How sweaty those walks. Sticky skin on sticky skin. And oh, the whispered poems between them, words as moist in the heat. Until that sixteen-something 'poet-singer', well, how he introduced himself, arrived. New boy at school. A year ahead of them, but he walked their route home. His house was on one of the side-streets that they often explored. So, he tagged along and somehow soon inserted himself between them and talked poetry, music, birds, so her bestie grew starry-eyed ... how she missed the skin on skin ... then ...

They had run way ahead, like wild goats up *their* hill while she struggled behind, slow runt that she was. When she finally reached the top, she could no longer hear their laughter. It had gone quiet, except for a distant bird trill. Then she saw them, her leaning against a large trunk, him leaning towards her, so, so close, as if it was just them, just them in the world.

She edged closer to hear him.

"I read the poems. You have talent, y'know. But your friend, uhm, I don't think so, and—and I don't think she understands birds."

And they kissed.

It was just her now, just her alone in the world.

Critic reads the rejected poem for the nth time, folds it small, smaller and smaller, and drops it into her drawer, then reaches for the whiskey.

A year later, an encounter. If anyone wrote *this* in a novel, she'd say it's contrived, Critic would later tell herself. It happens between the potatoes and the garlic on her rushed shopping just before the grocer closed. She's had a bad day. Her review was critiqued! Sure, the paper's editor was trying to be diplomatic, asking if she could tone it down a bit (tone it down! a bit?), saying that he'd read the novel himself and felt that hers was an unfair reading, so maybe she misread … etc, etc (misread!).

She's bagging potatoes. Under her arm, a folder of stuff. She keeps hearing that phone call with the paper's editor, and she's getting angrier and angrier. Potatoes hurled into the bag and she's just about to hurl them around anytime now—the nerve! You read the novel, yes, but I'm *a different reader* and you asked me, *me*, to review it!

The bag drops to the floor, then the folder—papers and potatoes scatter.

From the garlic at the end of the aisle, someone rushes to her side to help.

When all's rescued, the woman, it's a woman, hands her the final stuff from the floor, but not before staring at it.

"Oh, thanks, thanks."

"You okay?" Under a bright red hat with heavy black flowers, she sounds concerned, maybe a tad too solicitous. "Really okay?"

"Yes, yes, thanks," she says, quickly inserting the A4 sheet back into the folder.

The woman does not budge. "Something wrong?"

"I'm okay, thanks again," she says, returning to the potatoes.

The red hat with its black foliage still does not budge. Go away, sticky beak!

"Can I help?"

So, she looks up from the potatoes, finally looks at the face under the hat. Asian or Arabic or Mediterranean, no, she's not good with faces.

"I —" the face starts, then, "Never mind," and walks away, murmuring, "Take care of yourself."

What was all that about?

Then beyond the aisles, the red hat calls out, "Lost Bird."

"What?"

"Your poem … lost bird."

"Wh—?" But the hat is gone.

Between the potatoes and the garlic, Critic hesitates, then takes out the page that was rescued: near empty whiteness except for the tiny scribble.

> Morning blank blue
> cloudless, clean
> to write on

Critic ruminates. Red hat. Lost Bird. Her poem. But is it a really *a poem*? And that woman, the lost-ness about her—now, don't get sentimental. Wasn't she smiling as she called out beyond the aisles? She did seem worn out, though, exhausted, and didn't she shuffle along rather wearily? Wonder where she's from.

The three-line scribble has been sitting on her desk for a week now. Daily, she's stared at it. Lost Bird?

Again and again, she runs a finger on the eight words that she wrote, trying to figure out that encounter and what the woman saw. Had she looked at the clean whiteness, she would have seen *it* too. But she has a better idea! She picks up her mobile, she'll talk to The Poet, her friend, no, she must see her, it must be a visit, a surprise, she feels a rush in her chest! She'll make up for her silence, their silence, and she'll tell her she did read her book and liked it, loved it, and she'll take this poem and the story about the woman and the lost bird, she'll 'fess up, they'll have dinner and wine and talk and talk.

It will be all right again … arm in arm up their hill.

Oh, the things she wanted to say or do then and beyond, the could-haves and would-have-beens, the flights of fancy or desire, hurt or anger to fill up the space vacated by the past. But the past does not just up and go. Even if it does, there's always the shadow. But she does not see it.

I'm getting soppy, ugh!

She ruminates. Then decides against the wine, the dinner, the telling, the visit. She returns to her desk, to the problem review. Okay, I'll tone it down and meet that publication deadline. Happy now?

Fate contrives, as much as writers. Critic will come to this conclusion the next year. When she catches, by chance, a TV interview that glues her to the screen. Red hat! There's no mistaking *her*! So, fate arranges. *Fate and its own artifice.*

"Your book. Critics say this is autobiographical," Interviewer starts. "Is it?"

"Critics, yes, uhm … I write based on my own life, because I — I always feel uncomfortable about writing about others, y'know, with certainty, I mean, I'm afraid I'll get it wrong and what if I hurt, I'm rambling here … but there are writers who are so confident, fearless. But I wonder more about those who write about what others write, they're twice removed, but—but they write, and read, with such certainty, such authority … don't you ever wonder about this … about how we read what others write about others' lives—what do you think?"

Interviewer smiles. "I think I'm asking the questions."

"Sorry, of course."

"Okay, back to autobiographical—so why didn't you write a memoir instead of a novel?"

"Well, I'm a writer, invention is my trade, so, uhm, I prefer fiction."

"Indeed, one wonders about how a writer, like you for instance, finds the balance between your life and others' lives as you tell a story. But I'm more interested in how you balance writing about life in this home, *where you live now*, and in your first home. Correct me if I'm wrong, the way I read this novel (and she puts up the book for the TV viewers—Critic is stunned!), it seems you're always shuttling between two lives, two sensibilities, and between two languages too. You have parts here in your original language," and she runs her hand on the book cover. "I like that."

Critic moves closer to the screen. That's the book I reviewed a while back, that's *her,* the novelist, *her* at the grocer's! Red hat! Lost bird! Fate.

Interviewer leans forward, intimate now. "So, how do you blend your two homes in one book?"

"I'm just being myself, I guess—I have two homes and two languages, two lives as you say, so I just write who I am."

Interviewer nods but is not satisfied. She runs a hand on the book again, carefully as if she were reading Braille. "Such loss and grief—but how can one write emotions so raw without overdoing it?"

"Oh, did I overdo it?"

"That's not what I mean."

Awkward pause.

Novelist shifts in her seat, then asks, "How do you cry?"

Interviewer is taken aback.

"Do you overdo it?"

Interviewer is lost for words.

"How do your tears sound?"

Interviewer regains her composure and bats back the question: "How do your tears sound?"

"Unfortunately, not in English."

Interviewer laughs to hide her annoyance. "Ah, you cry in your first language. I get it—of course, we've just been talking about your original language. But remember, I'm asking the questions here."

Camera closes in on Novelist, as she breathes in deeply then out, with great difficulty this time, whole body exhaling, lifting shoulders, head, lifting the immense black flowers on her red hat, so they almost disappear from the screen. "I know. This is an interview. You ask the questions. About writing. But writing is bound with reading what's been written, right? Can't just be about how I write, but also about how you read my book." Another struggle to breathe. "So, how do I write, think, cry, laugh, sound? Certainly, not like you—so—so, it's important for me to also ask: how do you read what doesn't sound like you?"

Interviewer clears her throat, then firmly, "About your question earlier if you've overdone it, sorry, I didn't mean that. I'm interested in how you write raw emotion, especially grief, over dying, especially as you say it's based on your own life. So, let's run with your sticky question: How do you cry? How does anyone cry anyway? This is relevant to what I really want to ask: how do you respond to the reviews that say your novel is— is sentimental — "

"*Sentimental.* Interesting word. Easy word." The red hat bends towards the Interviewer, hiding the face underneath as it whispers, "Can I tell you a story?"

Critic is convinced. *Fate contrives, as much as writers.* And maybe that second encounter, albeit through TV, was poetic justice? No, don't go there. But she can't help thinking about it, worrying about it, having sleepless nights over it, even grieving over it. Indeed, how do we cry? That question took her aback too. And what is lost, what is found? How do we read it? She thinks she understands it now, the novelist's story at that interview, which she transcribed to read and re-read.

> Once upon a time, there was this strange creature from somewhere else. It was as large as the open field, tall as the sky, with feet that reached the depth of the deepest river. Ah, sooo large indeed. But small. Why, you ask. Because it kept itself hidden. Everyone said it was best kept hidden. And believe me, it had colours so bright, they hurt the eyes, and these colours, all sorts, were not really the right combination, like, you don't pair a deep purple shirt with shocking green pants, do you? Well, that was what everyone said. And listen to this, listen, it laughed and its laughter was so loud, but its cry was even louder, too loud and embarrassing, everyone said. So, it kept quiet. It had wings, oh yes, wings that spanned the distance from land to sea, to where it came from. That's why it was so large. It was connecting different lands and waters. But it took up too much space, stealing space from others, everyone said. So, it stopped flying, it stopped laughing, it stopped crying, oh that was hard. But you see, it felt the embarrassment of those around it. It grew embarrassed of their embarrassment, know how that feels? So, it decided to forget who it really was, where it came from. It even tried to forget its name: *Sentimiento*. Because it was loud, rough, unrefined, everyone said. It had to be streamlined. Or maybe set aside? Silent, small, hidden. And wait for this. Soon, everyone changed its name, called it *Sentimental*.

Critic reads it again. She remembers how something broke in her after that interview, which grew even more awkward. Probably why the program had to cut it short. The program's main presenter explained that it was old footage of an interview with the novelist who, sadly, died yesterday. Brain tumour. "She has no relatives here. So, her body will be flown back to her first home."

☾

Three years later, another date. Critic and Poet together again. Reconciled, well, sort of. They go through the motions, but they never talk about the whys and wherefores.

Again, they clink champagnes and sit down for the awarding.

Poet squeezes Critic's hand. Clammy. "I hope you win."

"Who knows," she says, squeezing back. "I don't do poetry, really."

"*You are a poet*—I've always known. Remember those days?" Critic squeezes harder. "That hill …"

Poet rearranges the hold, tucks her arm around the other's.

The hall dims and the emcee takes the stage.

Poet whispers, taps the book, "And *this* honours that novelist, poor thing. Glad you told me—you have to tell *that story* if you go up there, and you'll go up there. 'Lost Bird' indeed, good luck!"

Arm in arm again. Skin on skin.

Shortly, as the applause subsides, Critic-turned-Poet gathers the room with her eyes, then, "Thank you for this award. Thank you for believing in *this*," and holds up her first poetry book: *Lost Bird*. "But it's not really what is lost, is it? But what is found. So, what have I found?" She pauses, looks around the hushed room, suspends the moment, the audience raring to hear her revelation. She delivers. Tiny tremor in her voice, she tells the story of an encounter at the grocer's some years back, between the potatoes and the garlic, when a woman rescued her eight-word poem that fell from her folder, and how this woman called out,

174

"Lost Bird"—and this was how she found her voice. After that gift, she just kept writing poetry, even if she doesn't do poetry, really. "I'm a critic, as everyone knows."

Few chuckles around.

"Name her," her friend whispers to herself, "Name her."

"So, this book *Lost Bird* is my honouring of that gift, *my* found voice. It's difficult to move from critic to poet. Poetry's a different, difficult ball game altogether. But uncannily, it happened, and I'm grateful to *my* lost bird, *my* rescued one—" she's snagged by a catch in her throat. So, she breathes out, all air released to ripple the adulation of her audience who are, no doubt, convinced. Yes, as critic, she was fearless. But as poet now, her fearlessness is breathtaking.

"So, each time I wake up," she continues, "the morning is blue but never blank. *Because I have written.*"

Ah, this stiff-upper lip woman, some call her hard-hearted, now opening her heart, now brave enough to be vulnerable—oh, is she going to cry?

"So, thank you, judges, thank you, readers—for finding this lost bird with me," and she waves the book in the air.

The applause goes on and on.

As she leaves the stage, New Poet smiles at her friend in the front row. She'll tell her now, she'll 'fess up, she'll fill the silence from all these years.

But her friend cannot smile back. *Why did you not name the novelist?*

Back in her seat, the proud awardee links her arm with her friend's who hears not the dying applause, but something else: a bird hovering around carrion, about to land and pick.

The Poet

After *The Poet* by Lily Prigionero

LIZZ MURPHY

A photographer makes a study of the poet Walt Whitman
At a future time an artist makes a watercolour and ink
drawing from this image frames it hangs it in a café A
poet arrives at this same café for breakfast sits at the
back table under this Walt Whitman She eats and writes
and thinks In deep thought she rests her chin in her hand
A smiling man strides towards her: I'm sorry — I just
have to tell you — you look exactly like the picture
behind She turns to see Is surprised even though she
has taken notice of this portrait on many occasions (Oh
you again Walt always says) She is also pleased and she
says I'm trying (ironically) to do the same thing here
(write) Later she wishes she had a photo of herself chin-
in-fist in front of Walt-Chin-in-Fist Instead she googles
the original Whitman photograph and does her own
rendition from it in pencil She gets a blog post out of it
and a documentation of that particular day when bare
earth too slowly washed green and groves of sorry trees
curled their leaves early in the pandemic Meanwhile an
artist posts her painting of a man in another café who by
chance or not is another poet The first poet in a café
finds this painting striking the black-and-white tiled

foreground dramatic   the two turquoise ice cream posters like windows on to the world on a bright day They make the ochre walls and tablecloths glow The poet in the painting merges charcoal overcoat into charcoal pew One contented hand rests in the other on the table his face more studious There may be an actual window out on to the world and he could be gazing at life unfolding unravelling He might be drifting off into his own world the one in his head There is nothing on his table He has just arrived is waiting for coffee or a meal a simple cheese sandwich a bowl of the home-made ice cream Or he is already satiated Everything cleared away just him left sitting He may be a regular and the staff say: Oh he's just The Poet let him sit—he is finding his way with the world finding his way with words—some days it takes time let him have an extra serve The artist who has painted the splashes of light the lowering shadows the curiosities on the shelf high above his head could still be perched at the opposite end of that café with her easel and canvas or with just a camera to take the photo to paint from after She is a poet as well so we come full circle The painted scene could easily be during a pandemic when most people are at home self-isolating and those necessarily out are in need of socially-distanced succour from the essential workers providing food in eerily quiet cafés and staring out of their windows wondering where it will all end and who will get a poem out of it

Educating Nanette

SUSAN MIDALIA

The Sunday morning drive had been a long-standing ritual for Mr and Mrs Mullins and their daughter Nancy, who at the restless age of thirteen re-named herself the more sophisticated Nanette (*Mullins* would have to wait, she thought, until she married a Smith or a Jones). She also told her parents she had too much homework/had to study for a test/had to go to the library, to join them on this family outing. She didn't tell them that she couldn't see the point of their meandering through different suburbs that all looked the same: the bland brick houses and immaculate gardens, men mowing lawns or washing their cars, prim little girls playing hopscotch on driveways and boys doing stupid wheelies on the road.

The only moment, the enduring moment, that had wiped out her resentment—the tedious views, her mother's backseat driving, her father singing along to the radio (*Tie a Yellow Ribbon round the Old Oak Tree*, for goodness' sake)—was her glimpse of the university tower, poised elegantly above a lake. Her friend Deborah told her how she'd once climbed the winding stairs inside the tower, *just like a fairy-tale*, and how Nanette must do it too, she must go to university because her essays were always brilliant and she always topped the class in English, History and French (*the girly subjects*, some of the boys would sneer, wielding a slide rule or compass). Deborah's parents were both doctors and she played classical guitar and had been to Europe twice, but she didn't mind Nanette's cramped bedroom or the way Nanette's parents slurped their soup, then urged the girls to watch *Bellbird*. But Deborah *had* minded, an awful lot, when her mother kept correcting Nanette's vocabulary: *it's napkin, dear, not serviette ... it's dessert, not pudding*. She'd called her mother *a snob of gigantic proportions* and was grounded for a week.

No one in Nanette's family had ever been to university. Not her parents, nor a single aunt, uncle or cousin, and certainly not her older sister, who'd married the local policeman and had two girls and a boy in eight smug years.

Every time she saw the tower, Nanette's heart would go thump, thump, thump.

I will work hard and learn, she told herself. I might even win a prize.

Heading for seventeen and in her final year of school, still topping the class in her favourite subjects, Nanette was pleased to learn that, thanks to the new Labor government, university fees had been abolished. Her parents had always voted Labor and were now even more enthused by the party's rush to make the country *a much more decent place*, her father declared: getting rid of conscription and capital punishment, making health care affordable for everyone, not just the rich toffs. Her mother wasn't entirely convinced by the need for free universities, but her father nodded approval. *Never knock back anything if you don't have to pay*, he said.

And we'll have heaps of fun as well, Deborah insisted. She called it *being well-rounded*.

Their English tutor had snow-white hair falling to her shoulders and wore cheesecloth dresses that floated to the floor. She was a large woman given to theatrical gestures, a constant stream of smoking, and melancholy pronouncements on the anguished nature of love. She writes poetry, Deborah whispered, as if that explained the hair, the dress, the unsettling kind of sadness adrift in the foggy room.

Nanette's History tutor smoked a pipe, and in between studious puffs, would pontificate about *the rise of the West*, which seemed to mean endless battles, the planting of flags and bringing civilisation to the natives. (Nanette and Deborah much preferred the egalitarian impulses of the French Revolution, which they'd studied at school, although the severed heads on spikes had made them feel downright queasy.)

The French tutor, Mademoiselle Nicolette, spoke so rapidly that Nanette couldn't keep up.

Their first English lecture was held in a cavernous room packed with long-haired boys and girls in corduroy overalls or brightly coloured kaftans studded with tiny mirrors. The lecturer wore a tight fluffy jumper and would often raise his arms to reveal a wide strip of flesh above his jeans. My god, he's sexy, Deborah whispered, which made Nanette look down, embarrassed, at her prim brown skirt. She hardly heard a word of what fluffy jumper said.

That afternoon she went to the local op shop and tried on a leather miniskirt. She studied her knees carefully in the mirror. They were sturdy knees. Dependable, boring knees. But when she turned side on in the mirror, she was pleased with the shape of her behind. Curvy, but not too big. Or too small. As far as she could tell.

Deborah suggested going on a double date so that she and Nanette could lose their virginity at the same time. *In separate locations, of course*, she laughed. Nanette smiled, wanting to look brave, hoping to look ready. (She hadn't been ready for menstruation at the age of twelve, when her mother had merely handed her a booklet called *You're a Young Lady Now,* and told her not to let boys touch her.)

Nanette said none of this to her parents, of course. About a man's bare flesh and a double date and losing her virginity (she wondered why the first time meant *losing*). But she did show them the list of questions for her first English essay, to which they asked their own questions, their faces puzzled, their tone polite, about the meaning of *theme, symbolism* and *enhance.* Her mother released her from housework to give her more time to study. And while her father was bemused by her textbooks— he thought sixty pages of French grammar and vocabulary was fifty-nine too many, and *As I Lay Dying* sounded much too grim for the young—he conceded that a good education was her ticket to success. Meaning landing a good job, Nanette thought. A much better job than his work on the factory floor.

A different English lecturer—a thin, stony-faced woman who never once raised her eyes from her notes—told them about someone called F. R. Leavis. (Was this a man or a woman, Nanette thought, scribbling in her notepad. And why would someone call themselves by their initials?) The lecturer spoke in tweedy tones about something called *the great tradition* and the *morally educative purpose of literature.* Nanette tried hard to follow. She would have to check the reading list (a whole page of recommended articles and books!).

The next day, her English tutor (Nanette tried not to look at the woman's heavy breasts beneath her diaphanous gown) told them to *expunge* from their minds any notion of F. R. Leavis or the morally educative purpose of literature. She scoffed at what she called *self-congratulatory idealism* and *stultifying convention,* insisting instead on the need for *transgression, the breaking of social taboos.* She told them that *a book must be the axe for the frozen sea inside us.* From the corner of her eye, Nanette saw a boy and girl, both wearing bell-bottom jeans and sloppy jumpers, entwine their bare feet, then rub them together in a slow, languorous motion. She felt something swelling in her heart.

In the library coffee shop, where students discussed everything from existential philosophy to the latest hairstyles (crimped or shagged, but most definitely not permed), Nanette mentioned the couple in their class.

"They're bold, aren't they?" she said.

"I'd call them horny," Deborah said, and laughed. "Although …" Her face turned suddenly dreamy. "Maybe … sometimes … touch is enough."

"Enough for what?"

Deborah sighed. "To know that you're there. That you matter."

They sipped their coffees (they were learning to drink it black). Then Deborah nodded in the direction of a tall young man with a gaggle of young women at his table.

"That's Simon Winterbottom," she said. "He's the president of the Apathy Club. They couldn't care less about anything, apparently."

Nanette raised an eyebrow. "So how come they have a president?" she said.

Deborah smiled. "Good point," she said.

Nanette took a closer look. "And Simon What's-his-face seems to enjoy girls swooning all over him," she said.

Deborah laughed out loud. "An even better point," she said.

Halfway through the year, Nanette attended a lecture on the poetry of Robert Frost, delivered by the stony-faced woman. Stamping out words like quatrain and volta, rural and realistic, the lecturer sounded even stonier than before. Nanette had studied Frost at school and had been faintly repelled by all that folksy wisdom (she'd once joked to Deborah that Frost's poetry left her feeling cold). Now, wishing her friend was beside her instead of stuck in bed with flu, Nanette found herself yawning.

"Bored, are you?"

She jolted. There had been an empty space beside her, but now it was filled by a gangly young man with a head of wild brown curls. She noticed his dark green eyes, his bushy eyebrows. She noticed the hair on his wrist.

"There's another theory about yawning," he said, and leaned a little closer.

Nanette couldn't move. Didn't wish to move.

"A yawning person might be feeling angry," he said. "Is that how you're feeling right now?"

She looked away, then back again, into those dark green eyes.

"I'm feeling warm," she said, and blushed. "I mean … it's hot in this room, isn't it?"

The young man gave her a gap-toothed smile.

"I'm Michael," he said. "And I love the shape of your nose."

That night, Nanette and Michael lost their virginity in his narrow college bed. Lying scrunched up beside him and still feeling a little sore, she was also feeling—what was it? It hadn't been ecstatic or even a little thrilling, but still … she felt proud of her blood on the sheet. Quietly elated.

"I'll get better," Michael said, shyly. "I've been reading about it."

"We'll both get better," she said.

He nestled into her, nuzzled her neck. "I read something else," he said. "How the smarter you are, the older you'll be when you lose your virginity."

Nanette smiled. "Do you know the statistics for that?" she said. (Michael was studying maths.)

He began to stroke her hair.

"I heard some priest call virginity *a gift*," he said. "How you must give it to the person you marry."

Nanette felt bold. Almost wanton.

"Do you know the definition of a gift?" she said. "My friend Deborah learned it in anthropology. A gift is something you give without expecting anything in return."

She pressed her body into his.

"That's not my idea of sex," she said.

Michael laughed. "I knew you were smart," he said.

She thought of Deborah lying in a different kind of bed, a sick bed. She would visit her tomorrow with a bunch of flowers but she wouldn't tell her she'd lost her virginity. Not right away, at least. She didn't wish to make Deborah feel any worse than she already did, with her friend's hacking cough, blocked-up nose and *I'm just aching all over and I think I might die and please cheer me up from the doorway*.

Deborah. Who didn't care about cauliflower cheese for dinner or the proper name for pudding; who wasn't afraid to berate her snobbish mother; who'd urged Nanette to go to university, laughed at her jokes, and knew the truth about sex before Nanette could find the words.

Michael drew away from her. "What are you doing tomorrow?" he said.

Nanette smiled into his eyes. "I'm going to see my best friend," she said.

GINA MERCER

a crooked stack of books
waits on the weathered table
pile of possibility
for a friend who's thinking
of writing a new world

enduring form of women's piracy

passing books we love
hand to work-strong hand
sparking words mouth to mouth
fomenting gentle revolutions
making   stacks of our own

Note: This poem is written in the 'elevensies' form invented by Kerri Shying, a NSW poet of Chinese and Wiradjuri heritage. The form comprises 11 lines: 5 + 1 + 5, with the middle line used as the poem's title. (*Elevensies* by Kerri Shying, Slow Loris chap book series, published by Puncher & Wattman, 2019.)

In this 'elevensies', the middle line refers to 'women's piracy' as discussed by Susan Hawthorne at a digital publishing conference in Sydney, 2009. Susan spoke of women's often subversive tradition of sharing books as a way of connecting and growing a network of intellectual companionship.

Cowrie's Return

CATH KOA DUNSFORD

The ukulele festival starts with a jam, Wild Women Ukes leading it. They begin with a pōwhiri, one of Justine's Māori students, Ruby Topia, leading with the pūmoana, conch shell greeting, followed by Hirini Melbourne's rousing Nga Iwi E waiata, where all people are urged to join together as one, whatever their background or beliefs. It's powerful on the ukulele and the maestros provide a drum accompaniment. Gradually, Justine is building a strong network of musicians who contribute to the ukulele performances. She and Gloria had talked about this vision before, expanding the band so that a wide range of musicians from youth to elders can take part. The songs range from easy and popular to more difficult ones so that ukers of all abilities can take part. They always throw in a good selection of Māori and Pacific songs, from *Pōkarekare Ana, Tūtira Mai Ngā Iwi, Purea Nei, Te Aute, Hoki Mai* and a beautiful Hawai'ian hula song, *For You a Lei*, which was given to them by Cowrie. Her great uncle, Oscar Hyatt, a Hawai'ian music publisher in Honolulu, co-wrote the waiata with Johnny Noble. Justine had to spend time arranging it to be played by ukers, as it had difficult chords. Justine's voice soars over the notes like a tūī in flight, deftly flying over the jade river, between the tree branches, its tonal range never failing to delight listeners.

Harikoa community is catering the festival with spray-free produce from their gardens and delicious kai moana from the ocean licking the shores beside them. The trestle tables groan from the weight of the delicious food placed before the ukers. Roasted kumara and purple urenika, seafood chowder, raw fish salad, oysters glittering in their shells, plump and erotic. Green, orange, red and purple rainbow salads, slices of wild pig from the spit covered in warm, oozing gravy. Agria and Nadine potatoes freshly dug from the soil this morning, steamed with mint. Wild pestos made from garden herbs like Vietnamese mint, basil, Italian parsley, garlic chives, lemon balm and healing kawakawa leaves, blended with local olive oil and ground macadamia nuts from a nearby farm. They live in the land of plenty. But not all share these resources. The ukers are donating the profits from the festival to the homeless and those with less access to such resources. Most live in the cities, some from their own whānau, who lost connection to the land and the ability to take care of their families and those they love. It's a crime that so many are in need in a country with such rich natural resources. Factory farming had destroyed the old cottage industries, as it had done all over the western world. People are forced off the land and can so easily become destitute. Some of the songs talk about this. But not enough. Gloria feels there is a gap to be filled. Love for the land and the people as well as well as for individual lovers.

The Māori Hawai'ian uker, Cowrie, who'd taken the Plucky Riffer workshop the day before joins them. She squeezes in beside Gloria. Her black wavy hair surfs wildly from beneath her island fedora hat. She's a bit of a pirate figure, with bold, sterling silver rings in her ears and a mother-of-pearl oyster shell turtle around her neck. Gloria could imagine her hauling in a net through the waves, parrots perched on her shoulders. "Aloha, kia ora. Looking forward to your workshop."

Cowrie places a large bowl of steaming seafood chowder in front of her and glances at the group.

"We thought you'd be too advanced for that," says Gloria. "You've always got new things to learn with the ukes. I've been so keen to follow my Māori and Hawai'ian heritage with our Pacific waiata and writing riffs for traditional songs that I've neglected the likes of Fleetwood Mac. Not that I'd ever get over seeing Stevie Nicks singing live in San Francisco when I was working on Te Māori in the eighties. It was a blast. I was taken by her soul. It soars through her singing. I hope you'll match her today."

Justine looks a bit taken aback.

"No worries," says Gloria. "Our Justine has her own soulful style. You'll love it."

"Are you double riffing that amazing intro?" asks Cowrie.

"Yeah, with my mate Sophia."

Gloria introduces them. "And this is Justine our teacher. You can blame her if we stuff it up."

Cowrie laughs. She glances across the table. "No worries, Justine. It's their responsibility to get their riffs right. You're off the hook. My uke students in Hilo and Kona try this trick too. Don't let them get away with it."

"I try my best to keep them in check," replies Justine. "But Sophia and Gloria are not easily trained. They have vibrant minds of their own and a wicked humour to boot. We work as a team and I know they always give their best."

"Very noble of you, Justine. She didn't keep us in check at Geraldine Ukefest. We went wild." Sophia grins.

Gloria turns to Cowrie. "So where are you bound after the festival?"

"I'll find a wee bach to hang out for a few days by the sea then go west and visit the rellies in the Hokianga. I fancy a bit of surfing and lazing about, maybe a bit of gardening and reading before I face the cuzzies who will all have so many questions about our Hawai'ian rellies. I've drip fed them information from the Big Island but I know they'll be all over me in person."

That doesn't sound too bad a plan, thinks Gloria, secretly. "Haven't they met yet?" asks Gloria.

"No. We knew a few tales but I had to return to Hawai'i to get the full whakapapa. It started on a journey in search of my great grandfather, Apelahama, who came out to Aotearoa from Hawai'i and it grew when we discovered my great Uncle Oscar Hyatt joined a travelling band as concert pianist. He was African Kiwi. A strain of the whanau that only emerged after some hard research. Long story. He went all over Aotearoa, played a while in Fiji then the band arrived in Honolulu and never wanted to leave. He stayed and married into an indigenous Hawai'ian 'ohana. He started one of the earliest music publishing houses in Hawai'i, kept playing the piano at a local hotel and all over the islands and mainland, then he learned the ukulele and got hooked. He paired up with composer Johnny Noble and together they wrote the famous hula song, *For You a Lei*, which we played yesterday. By the way, Justine, I like the arrangement you did for your students. Could I take this back for mine?"

Justine is honoured to be asked and dips into a folder and hands over her arrangement. Their eyes meet. Cowrie sees a woman who knows music from the heart and soul. It emerged through her arrangement of the song but she now sees it written in her eyes. Justine is shy and looks down at her music again. Cowrie reaches her hand over the table and touches Justine's wrist warmly. "Mahalo nui loa, Justine." Justine, who dislikes open displays of affection, tries not to withdraw her hand. Yet she feels an electric charge of energy and creativity, just as Cowrie did all those years ago when first touching a turtle in Hawai'i. Cowrie feels it too.

Our Pacific Paradise is an inspiring workshop. Cowrie sits in the front row to take it all in. Justine, indeed, sings like a tūī. Cowrie recalls her mother, Mere, telling her a whakataukī or proverb about the tūī as a songbird having the sweetest voice of all. The great orators would try to emulate the tūī. She feels transported into the Waipoua Forest, which she walked through as a child. Ka ngaro reoreo tangata, kiki e manu. No human voice. Only the song of birds. "Fern fronds swaying in subtropical breezes, Doing just whatever will please us." Justine's blond hair flows in waves under her black fedora, like the surfing lava of Pele flowing down from Kīlauea Crater into the crashing sea below. She remembers a unique painting of Pele with blond hair, her strong, powerful body flying through the crater, evoking stars of lehua blossom in her wake.

Cowrie leans forward, riffing. Sophia and Gloria uke well together, like the warp and weft of one cloak, interweaving beautifully with Justine's powerful, heavenly voice. "Feel aroha in the breeze." Cowrie is pulled up by Ranginui, high into the sky. She soars over the land, past Cape Reinga, glances down at the wild place where the Tasman and Pacific oceans meet, feels pulled by the power of spirit. They say this is the richest part of the ocean, breeding new life, as the oceans surge together. Whales and dolphins, turtles and sharks, krill and prawns all join in kotahitanga, feeding and nourishing themselves. The pull of the oceans is where creativity spirals, as one meets the waves of the other, crashing surf with no shore to land on. They join forces, ocean to ocean, in a passionate surge of spirit. Two worlds meeting as one. Fusing, wave upon wave upon wave. A tsunami of erotic power and creativity felt by the fish that swim in a frenzy around the curling peaks of spume. The sun sparks off the dazzling water, turned silver by its beams. Ranginui swoops down, sweeping up Cowrie, just as she begins to tip the waves, dive into the depths. Ranginui has other plans for her. She is pulled upward, swiftly, rescued just in time, her wing tips still wet with water.

Paige

PAULINE HOPKINS

As I pushed I knew that this baby was not meant to survive. The pains of labour should not have to be experienced when death is already waiting; beckoning with an outstretched clawed finger.

Yet I pushed and pushed. The sweat was moistening my brow and I could feel the cotton sheet clinging to my exposed back. I felt grotty and ugly and in pain. I wanted it all to be over and to be rid of this ordeal.

Yet when she emerged Paige was not dead. To be sure, her intestines were exposed to the world, arranged in neat loops as they should be but without the covering of skin. I laid a clean gauze bandage over the gaping hole and lifted my baby over my shoulder, patting her lightly on her back.

"Mum, don't hold me like that," she said. "Don't hold me vertically or my insides will fall out."

So instead, I cradled her in my arms horizontally and rocked her back and forth, singing soothing gentle notes.

My baby is alive and talking, I contemplated, wondering at this miracle.

I prepared for a visit to hospital wondering if this gorgeous creature could perhaps live and shake off the shackles of death that still hung ominously around the room.

Yet, accompanied by death was the tune of life, both mournful and sweet, like the song of a nightingale. I feared for this beautiful, talking, newborn child.

Her skin was pale but supple, with none of the redness that often accompanies first entry into the world. Bar a few almost invisible wisps, her head was bald of hair. But her eyes! Her eyes! She looked right at me, piercing my heart and soul with her honest gaze.

"It's ok, Mum," she said. "Even when I'm dead, it will be ok."

"It's not ok," I sobbed. And I stood, a sweaty, near-naked mother, face laced with tears, holding a wizened newborn baby with the freshness of infancy that would never know childhood.

I went through the motions: sort of got dressed, bundled up a harried bag of clothes and supplies, all under the watchful gaze of Paige, whose eyes followed my frantic movements with the calmness of the Dalai Lama.

"Are you some sort of God, some angel?" I questioned, as I picked up my newborn and took her out to the car.

"I come from you."

The seat which should have held a sleeping newborn baby instead held Paige: eyes wide open, fully alert to what was going on around. When I stopped at the traffic lights, the rear view mirror showed she was staring right at me.

"I love you Mum."

"I love you too Paige."

At the hospital, the intimacy was removed. Suddenly Paige became another baby in distress, an object to be treated and manipulated by the best that modern medicine had to offer. I can't remember consenting to anything, but in minutes there was a tube, a mask, injections, machines ... Where had my baby gone?

"A home birth, in this situation, no wonder ..." I heard someone mutter.

Then it was my turn. I remember being held down—a man with hairy arms—the smell of one of those sickening hospital chemicals that instead of cleanliness spelled control. The white light overhead, blinding me.

"Paige. Paige!"

Then nothing but whiteness.

I wake to a sterility that is deadening as well as institutional.

"Where is my baby?" I demand.

I eventually get the obvious explanations: you do realise, of course, that your baby was born with incurable deformities … with such intestinal damage, there was really not much the doctors could do … who can say why these things occur … perhaps it is God's will?

I ask to see my baby. She is wheeled in, in a hospital cot, swaddled. I quickly unwrap her, free her arms, let her legs fall apart.

"There you go, darling Paige," I murmur.

"Thanks Mum," comes the reply. My baby winks at me and smiles. And then shuts her eyes.

Forever.

Morundah
(or Lunatic Fringe)

KERRYN HIGGS

Odd. To think of coming from fields of daisies
and labyrinthine pumpkin vines
a squat child, awed and beguiled
by open skies over the land
star-book in hand, no less a mystery.

To think of coming from years
of second best, contemptible, a woman
of poor family
(sister to an unruly brother
who inherits the place of a man).

To think of coming from a mist
of unbelonging, unacceding
never at home, always in mute revolt
inducted into a slot
given a code to live by
located, placed
but not quite fixed.

To think of coming from a harsh and alien world
unrelieved by knowledge of its shape
or mine

into this place
the fire burned down at midnight
to a point where I perceive my plight in detail
and in a certain solidarity
on the lunatic fringe.

Alive

SUE INGLETON

I open the venetians one by one. If its a sun morning Im angry that I didnt get in here earlier. Missed all that heat. Should leave them open at night. Then I get nervous exposed to next doors. Theyre very nice. Young couple but it's not them its the man who might come in the side gate. I cant lock it needs a padlock. I lose keys and cant remember combinations and then when Im on the other side its locked and I think why the hell did I lock it so stupid so paranoid who cares. I open the venetians. This is repetitive. Morning activity. Dont be frightened youre not in a rut youre not stuck here forever but where else would I be if not here. Cant afford to move now. Too expensive and where to? This suits I might as well live here as anywhere I suppose I might as well die here as anywhere. I imagine where Ill die. In my bed on the back verandah falling off as I strain my neck to see if the tanks full or empty tank empty if Ive left the hose running and forgot I put the stove alarm on but then I wander away and never hear it and in the middle of the night I sit up and gasp the bloody hose I didnt turn it off and I get up and throw on a jumper although of late I wear my clothes to bed as the house is a refrigerator. Theres no insulation in the walls nothing but spiders webs and they have no star ratings I could line the whole outside with another layer of something corrugated irons all the go up here they pop up everywhere better than the horrible geejaygardinerhomes that spread like a virus. This is a heritage town or should be. Greed all around just plain greed from the council the developers the cheap bricks cheap facades. Why do I care so much Im angry all the time with everything thats so unjust think joyful think happy happiness dalai lama stuff couldnt read that book I like my crime fiction but not bloody pdjames god ramble ramble and then I heard an interview with Val McDermid and she sounded wonderful some writers festival thats another thing writers festivals sometimes I think writers should be seen on the page and not heard theyve all become talking books themselves. Ghastly. Val McDermid talked well though but then I read her hated her writing. Theres a conundrum and Hilary Mantel sounds like a twee strange child/adult voice how could she sound like that and write such brilliant stuff. But she talked brilliance she doesnt judge her characters I wonder if she judges people. The phones ringing but I cant find it must be in my bag or coat with my bag in the bedroom under the pillow Im draining my brain functions into the phone I should turn it off but in the middle of the night Im awake and checking on weather in Beijing because its where my daughter lives with her Chinese husband and their two babes I never see two hours behind just back past Adelaide but ever so much higher than that. We live on a ball Earth is a ball round round the shape of the ovum of a golf ball of sago of jaffas.

When I began I thought Id change the world but I too soon ended up changing nappies. Why am I living in this strange place my true friends are far away when you live where no one knows who you were its hard and you begin a life again without any of the good bits to wear on your sleeve and you make new friends but they never go deep they never get under the skin, how could they youre not going to retell your life to everyone and in the end you dont care and you deliberately cover it up and become supercilious and so life and friends and things that fill the day are superficial to your heart and soul and routine becomes fearful because once there was madness and surprises and phone calls from agents provocateur and that phone call was from the hardware store to tell me theyve accredited the refund to my account for $4.80. Today is worth $4.80 is that all that will happen today?

I open the venetians one by one. The one over the glazed door the one over the dining table that belonged to mother that I left out on the verandah too long and it opened up the cracks, opened up a bit like mother in the end and now I have the same cracks almost identical cracks in the skin. They come in the night and amaze you in the morning. And all the creams from Oreal will not flatten them out. The best thing I can hope for is to be seen only by candlelight. Rain is falling this morning soft rain silently floating down when what this town needs is a downpour of biblical proportions to save it from drought. Still the rain drops falleth like a mercy from heaven and the flowers that are leftover from summer and autumn lift their sweet heads and drink and there's the grass that disappeared in the dry coming out bold as brass grass cannot die grass. Grass and cockroaches will survive and we will pass. We all will pass the thought that my daughter will die the grandchildren will die they will all come to their death day and what will they look like where will they be may the gods give them ease for I will not see it for hopefully I will not have to see it but it will come its more guaranteeable than the sunrise. There is a sun out there somewhere today. And I shall walk today. Rain or shine my knees are needing help the pain is always there on a walk my doctor says its good that youre in the system now being on public health because it takes a long time. She is referring to an inevitable knee operation somewhere in my future Im in the system because I had an arthroscopy keyhole stuff and cleaning out rubbish its just rubbish in there said the surgeon. Garbage knee have I used you as a waste disposal but I read a lot and rubbish it seems is accumulating all over my body and brain Im positively toxic like Helen in the tai chi class. These are the legs and knees that ran up walls and jumped huge cable reels that danced that twisted around my neck that wrapped around his body and couldve broken his back in the spasms of orgasmic delight.

Gazing across the grey welfare carpet. Theyve certainly rearranged this place. All broken up now into little sections with different waiting chairs some covered in cloth others molded plastic grouped by colour guards and people who help you grab you as you enter get your CRN all with iPads which they finger finger scoop scrape push TOUCH. In front of me there stands a woman of giant proportions two babes hang off her legs her hair is dirty she wears legging things which cling to every kilojoule a throbbing body of woman and she is angry. They are treating her respectfully calmly and soon they will place her over on the left to sit and wait to be looked after. She has no temper left for her children. There is an armed guard watching the whole thing. I smile at her across the abyss of have and have not.

I frequently ice my cakes whilst they are still warm disastrous results each time the icing soaks into the cake the cake looks depleted. I make them for the charity stalls. I dont make them completely they are always Greens cake mixes which get cheaper to buy the further away from town you get. My cake always looks awful yet the ladies thank me profusely and cut it up to sell as pieces and surprisingly it tastes fine and is moist inside. Moist. What an uncomfortable word moist just has to always end up in the mind as a womans sexual gateway ever ready like the battery waiting to be turned on. If it stops raining they will have the stall tomorrow if it doesnt Ill be left with a strange glazed carrot cake.

Desperate to have a slice this afternoon with a cup of chai tea I work out that I can do this if I cut up the whole cake and wrap each piece in gladwrap and present on a plate there I already did it for you ladies. Yum carrot cinnamon Ill regret this and I do.

You just have to give up wheat and sugar says Carol who has the body of a stick but a lovely face and a golden heart. Now she is one from my past one that I can sit with and talk not necessarily reminisce because we know it all now but we can talk about this and that and laugh and laugh the humour of letting it all go and we can be angry with the government because our politics were molded in the same cauldron of feminism so long ago. We are girls together women together our lined faces and grey silver hair reflect our experience back to us and neither of us sees the other as past it. Both of us see the younger one in our minds memory see the hungry flashing eyes the yearning mouths waiting to speechmake and change our world and we did too. She is happy to let it go but Im not. She has her art and no one can interfere with that. I cannot rest easy when my personal creativity is still the wild woman bringer of change I was once called the Loki of transformation that hasnt gone away. Time time I cant meditate I cant do tai chi Im floating in the primordial soup I need to drain the tub.

Joe floated into my mind the other afternoon. Youre a real gentleman my mother would say flirting with him and he loved it she felt safe flirting with him because us kids were always around and she knew she would never leave an opening. How fragile she was for men breakable compliable crushable usable deceivable learn to put them way up there above her their minds their decisions she was a true Victorian slave only good at raising kids she loved raising kids but the trouble is that we all grew up and then she disliked our choices our partners even our children especially when I had one born out of wedlock it would choke in her throat the word grand daughter my lovechild she came later in my life she came through and completed my motherhood now shes in China and has old Chinese women to nan her babes not me they will never know me my face my soft silver hair my loving arms empty of them the damned phones ringing and its seven oclock and itll be some incomprehensible person talking rubbish down the line to me about solar panels theyll stop that now because the government are so stupid theyve put an end to free power for the people I made the investment and have panels on my roof but now they say they wont pay me what they promised what can they do come and pull them off Ill shoot the bastards if I could only find the gun oh yes the gun from way back hidden somewhere no bullets but itd frighten the beejezus out of an unwanted invader on my roof.

Such a mess we are in such evil is abroad
                         [she searches, finds what she's looking for.]
                                  [lights a cigarette.]
I dont smoke
                         [draws lasciviously, expertly on the fag.]
Foul habit
                         [she observes the smoke curling away.]
At least something is moving

we come to the light

berni m janssen

       thunderheads pummel sky black
       a lean of colour
       wind pushed cries harbour in the squalling
       flap of gulls homing
       her voice is a scrap sprayed
       into a quiet destination

Black is the sky as it waits for the reign of stars.
Black are the clouds weighted with rain.
Black were the thoughts dusted with drought.
Backed up,   black,   the horizon.
Her thoughts drop,   small seeds puff the earth,   blackening.
All reign to rain.

               Thoughts empty as the dams fill.

That her gaze is astute, is neither memory nor habit.

       the rain a fall of thought, a soft declension, when
       mists, she
       all day rain
       a cloak a veil a comfort stroke, spoke she
       a soak of feelings
       a precipitate action

she fall   shower fall   spit spit fall   shower she
as spit spot soft spoke shower,   a sentence on the earth.

She registers the forms in their complexity
of light and shadow,   high and low,   line and point,   complexion.

    weather of poetry

dreams pace her blood, insistent, unspoken

    albino, milky, creamy, frosty, bleached,

between the eye and the page a gulf that she has
on occasion,   fallen   into
sometimes   to float   sometimes

She rests on the brink of the abyss, with an acceptance
of the small gestures words are
    in the vast regions of a page,   like   the footfall of insects
                on sand in the desert.

She is uncertain of how stories are made to hold,
when the murkiness of distinctions
    are amplified in the abyss.

    bruising howl windward
    clang bone stormdeaf
    vocal stroke
    air for ear vermillion
    corrupt magnolia fleshes sky

Let the lumber of words worn,   too weighty,   too ingrained,
    dissolve.

She would that words fly into the wind, tattered leaves,
    a spill of sentence, where a murder of crows picks them clean.

boat mouths pitching
suck and splice
ur and caress
sea floods pause   moments wayswing

Night has unfolded her skin, unlocked her bones, emptied her of
sound. She no longer echoes.

Silence is returning her.

A cartographer would have pleasure in her sense of the lines
and folds of earth,
the way her feet feel into the rhythm of the land.

She walks the land into her cells and allows their stories to dwell.
Rock, uplifted and sharp;   leaf dry disintegrating,   distracted
roots,   aired,   haunted,
sand, the dissolution of time; and   always   the possibility of grasses.

dewdamp fingerfrost spikes, spritely winds etching cold,

This with that goes, so we know. A knowledge descends,
hand to hand, mouth to mouth,   and we resuscitate,

rosy, flush, blush, cherry, carmine, madder, flame, rouge,

Breath and horizon, ground and vision.   Essentials in being.

The garden spruiks a spike of green.
Birds kindle a cheery clause, scribing a harmony.
Lizards tongue leaves, sipping drips.
Clouds roil, trees breathe, dust dampened
smell of rain, heart seeps, and your
toes tango, fingers leap, to cosset
the small green fertility, your memory,
your love, the grass, the orchard, your harbour.

orange, ginger, amber, lemon, honey,
saffron, mustard, lime, emerald,
leafgreen, olive, leafy,

We find in beauty a home. This soul our casa we come to.
We come to the light. We find a rainbow.

Duckegg blue, peacock, indigo, lavender, heliotrope,
violet, plum, aubergine, lilac, amaranth, mulberry

Her skin opens, pressed by a word. A yield to infinity.

Get Back In

ANGELA BUCKINGHAM

*She reached out to me. She offered her hand as if from a boat—
lost in darkness already. The palm of her hand, very white, as she
leaned out to me.*

What I was doing was foolish.

Risky.

Who swims away from a boat into nothingness?

Someone who knows the boat will sink.

How did I know that boat would sink?

After my mother told me there was an instant decision. I wouldn't
go back for the funeral. I put down my phone, felt heavy, but
didn't have time to shift it. It was Sunday. Noisy full with the
kids, friends, barbeque lunch, dropping a snow globe that
shattered into a million pieces, packing school bags, washing, late
night clothes folding. It was when I lay down, in my welcoming
bed, after my beloved had kissed me good night, that I realized
I wouldn't sleep. That I realized the weight was still there. I saw
her reaching out to me. I remembered the whiteness of her hand.

Miranda Hobbs. Dead. We are the same age, were the same
age. We went to school together. For me she'd died years ago.
But there was no funeral for that quasi-death, no recognition, no
moment. People called it a miracle. It wasn't a miracle.

My mother always liked Miranda. We were the same height, same weight, same colour, both did reasonably well at school. She had curly hair and was better at netball. But neither of those things made the difference. I remember the long ago night, the night that made the difference.

We were at the Uni Bar. It was dingy. Dirty. Perversely, the décor suggested the sole consideration in construction had been easy to clean: lino floors, white teflon walls, and fluorescent lights. Maybe that's why the house lights were never on. The only light came from behind the bar, the lights above the pool tables or on the stage if there was a gig. That night there was a band. It was too loud for me, even back then, and too hot. So we were sitting outside, on the concrete blocks. We could hear the band just fine in the warm night air. I still didn't like the music, an anthem to punching. But Miranda knew all the words. Drinking our beers. Smoking. Hanging out. We talked shit about the arrest of a man for the Backpacker Murders. About girls who hitch-hiked. Their bodies found in the forest not far from town. We were pissed. These murders ended our preferred form of transport. Cheap, often fun and only occasionally creepy. There were five of us sitting on those concrete blocks. In the dark. Five girls. Alive. Michelle and Jackie and another girl whose name I never thought I'd forget but I've forgotten. Drinking lots of beers. Together.

I also don't remember the name of the guy who came over. He had very fat cheeks, which made the top of his head look a lot narrower than the bottom. He accentuated this by shaving around his head leaving antennas of wiry curls sticking out at the top. He was weird looking. But that isn't why I didn't like him. He was a tool. He used to sell drugs at an underground bar called the Circus. I loved the Circus with its tiny dance floor, the mirrored walls and the tradition of the cops running down the front stairs and us all tearing up out the back stairs into the alleys. Anyhow, one night there, Fat Cheeks told me to never buy pills 'cause you don't know where they come from. He pointed out we were a fucking long way from Colombia so I should never buy cocaine. He had talked a lot about what I should and shouldn't do without inquiring if I wanted to do anything at all. So when he came over to us, interrupted our conversation, and offered some random pills at a bargain basement price, I politely declined. He didn't remember me. But that wasn't the moment when Miranda and I split 'cause she turned down the pills too. The other three swiftly made the purchase. He was gone. I never saw him again. Ever.

Miranda and I had a lot in common. We both liked the same guy. He'd broken up with me only a few weeks before. We both thought he was a very talented artist. He was quiet enough that he could be whoever we wanted him to be. Maybe Miranda and I imagined his inner workings differently. He didn't come between us. That night there was no jealousy because he was inside, in the dark, dancing furiously, throwing his slight body about. For all that we obsessed about him, neither Miranda or I even bothered to say good night to him when we left. He would have been surprised if either, or both, of us had pushed through the mass to say goodbye. He had no responsibility for us nor us for him. But we did to each other.

We piled into the car with Michelle driving, Jackie in the front seat, the girl I've forgotten, me and Miranda in the back. The car felt full cause we were all making a lot of noise, more loud music, and stuff, backpacks, sleeping bags. I have no memory of where we thought we were going. It was very late. Michelle wasn't worried about being pulled over cause she said she hadn't had that much to drink but the pill was clearly having some impact cause as we drove she opened the car door for a little air. She drove along with her car door hanging open. Even after all my beers that registered. But it wasn't conscious risk assessment. I was doing a lot of stupid things then. Stupid drugs, stupid sex, stupid games like shoplifting scavenger hunts, swimming in other people's pools, rock climbing, breaking onto the rooves of office buildings, hiking up to the edge of bushfires, before we stopped hitchhiking to anywhere … We were so bored. We needed risk. Still the open car door registered.

But the door hanging open wasn't the thing that made me do it. I didn't want to get out after the open door. Then we came to the bridge. I was leaning over the front seat, trying to change the music. There it was before us—lit up in the darkness. Orange glowing in the night. Four long lanes crossing the lake. Not one other car on it.

The bridge was important. It divided our town into North and South. We were from the South. We met people from the North but never made friends with them. It was too far away, too many bus routes required to have any sort of regular contact, the sort of contact necessary for friendship. There it was bathed in gold. An expanse. Beyond it blackness.

There was no way I was crossing the golden bridge. The car had to stop. Yelling at them, "Stop the fucking car!" Michelle singing loudly, out of tune, was not stopping. I threatened to empty my guts on the back seat of her mum's Ford. Then she stopped. Screeched to a halt. I threw open the door, crawled over the girl I've forgotten and scrambled up the verge.

None of the other girls cared. The pills must have been no care pills.

Except Miranda. "No! What are you doing? There's nothing around here."

That had not occurred to me. "I'll walk. It's cool."

"You're twenty kilometres from home."

Miranda was wrong. Years later I looked on a map. I was only fourteen kilometres from home. There is a big difference between fourteen kilometres and twenty kilometres. But standing there I had no idea how far I was from home. So distance was irrelevant.

I was there looking at the light of the bridge, deciding to walk off into the darkness.

"Dumb bitch, some beefhead in a ute will pick you up, drive you into the bush, rape you, chop you in bits and bury you. Get back in the car. Throw up if you have to but don't go off into the dark." Miranda was worried about me. Maybe it was just the earlier talk of the Backpacker Murderer. Maybe it was something else. For her it was okay to drink or take pills or fuck some guy in the toilets but walking off into the dark was insane.

She leant out to me. I stood on the side of the road. She looked at me. I looked at her. We saw each other. Our sight lines were straight and focused. We both considered danger, being raped, chopped up and buried in the bush. Death. It is a big thing to realize in a small moment. As she strained to reach me, we both knew. But knowing was irrelevant.

Breaking the parallel sight lines, I shook my head. I couldn't get back in that car.

Miranda held out her arm, stretching out her very white palm, leaning over the girl I've forgotten. White palm. Miranda was trying to save me. Michelle, in the driver's seat, was clearly bored by it all. She drove away. Back door open. Miranda staring at me, hanging out her arm as if she could reel me in. There was acceleration, laughing, screaming, the door closed.

Off they went, with my bag, my purse and my six-pack of beers.

And I turned into the dark. I decided not to walk along the road because I was scared of the guy in the ute or the Backpacker Murderer or generic bad guys. I figured if I walked in the shadows no one could see me. True, I couldn't see anyone either, but no one could choose me as his victim if he couldn't see me. I crossed the multi-lane highway, pushing my way into the trees lining the road. I walked.

I couldn't have made it far but I swear I didn't hear the car swerve or see the car smash through the bridge barrier.

I followed my feet, looking at each step, hearing the crack of the sticks, the harsh grating of the dry grass.

I was not long gone, when they went over the side, not into the lake but smashing onto the exit ramp. How can you not hear that? When it is so late, so dark, so quiet?

I didn't hear it. I didn't know I was right. I still had a long way to go through the night, finding the bike path and walking to the base of the mountain. At the underpass, I hesitated. A man-eating monster could be sleeping under there. I wouldn't want to wake him up because for such disruption he may change his diet and eat me. So I clambered back up, across the road and kept going. One step following another. Listening for threats too easily imagined. One foot. Then the next. The darkness washing out to a cool blue. Out of the scrub and onto the neatly manicured lawns of my parents' suburb. Jumping the fence. Seeing our house. Opening the back door into my room. And there was my mother. Sitting on my bed. Crying.

I was ready for a fight. It was too late or too early, not the right time to be getting home. I geared for self-justification. But she hugged me and cried and cried and cried. I could only think how hungry I was.

Everyone says it was a miracle they didn't die. But they did. None of them was who they were before they went across the bridge. Even the girl I've forgotten had completely changed. I went and saw all of them in the white purgatory of hospital. I sat for days next to Miranda. Imagining I was wrapped up like her. Waiting for some sign of life. Remembering her hanging out of the car, saying, "Get back in. You dumb cow. Get back in."

When Miranda got out of hospital, she learnt to walk again and talk. But she was slower. She didn't remember lyrics. She didn't like any boys. She didn't talk about anything much.

We never again drank beers or sat out in the warm night air or drove in a car together. She didn't graduate when I did. She's not even in the school photo. Maybe she was not as nothing as I thought. I don't know if she ever laughed again or had sex or ate a delicious meal or slept in the bush or lazed in hot bath until it was cold. She stayed with her mum when I left town. We didn't do reunions.

And now she is dead, in a way that everyone recognizes. I didn't even ask my mother how she died. It can't have been an adventurous death caused by flamboyance or ignored risk. Mum would have mentioned that. I'll ask next phone call. My mum will know how she died this time. My mother always liked Miranda.

Wimmera

JORDIE ALBISTON

where am I going until I am there
against the Wimmera sky   this travel
is ever   this travel is larger than
you or I   they go by so fast those scads
of paddock   ubiquitous rust buckets

stuck in the wheat but that's more or less death
I guess   bitumen stretches / sweats on &
on   & where am I going & where have
I gone   this travel always much more than
me   the eucalypts passing say calm   calm

but even the rocks here come to harm   words
& flies hum through my head & something's tired
perhaps even dead   a black snake does un-
does itself somewhere   & then I hear it
one last breath   but that's just life   more or less

Notes on Contributors

Angela Buckingham
Angela Buckingham has written for television, theatre and children's literature. She authored the books *Powerful Princesses*, *Courageous Queens* and *Lawless Ladies*, all collections of short stories about moments of crisis and triumph in real women lives. Together they form the Historical Heroines series published by Five Mile. She is currently the writer-in-residence with The Shift Theatre, after the 2022 production of her play *#NoExemptions*. She is a graduate from the Victorian College of the Arts.

Angela Costi
Angela Costi is the author of five poetry collections/books including *An Embroidery of Old Maps and New* (Spinifex Press, 2021). The *Relocated* arts project, for which she was writer-in-residence at the former Kensington Public Housing Estate, received the national award for community innovation, 2002. In 2009, she travelled to Japan as part of an international collaboration involving her poetic text *A Nest of Cinnamon*. She lives on Wurundjeri land. Her heritage is Cypriot.

Anne Ostby
Anne Ostby is an author and journalist from Norway, with 12 books for young adults, children, and adults. For the last 30 years,

she has lived and worked as a writer in nine different countries. She currently resides in Pakistan. Her writing frequently covers questions of identity and encounters between cultures, and explores the roles and challenges of women in different societies.

Aviva Xue

Aviva Xue is a feminist and teacher, with a Masters in English Literature and the writer of stories, essays and poems in both English and Chinese. Her book, *Weibo Feminism: Expression, Activism and Social Media in China,* was published by Bloomsbury in 2022. She is daring like a leaping cat and loves experimenting with new things. She is meticulous like Australian waxflowers – tiny yet with serious blossoms.

berni m janssen

berni m janssen is a maker (poems, performances, multi-disciplinary projects, preserves and more) living and working on unceded Dja Dja Wurrung Country. She often makes work with musicians, performers and visual artists. *between wind and water* was published by Spinifex Press (2018). Her most recent work, *ENA*, was performed at JOLT Arts and published by Hullick Studios (2022).

Bulbul Sharma

Bulbul Sharma is a painter and writer based in New Delhi. Her artworks are held in the collections of the National Gallery of Modern Art, Lalit Kala Akademi and Chandigarh Museum as well as in private collections in India, UK, USA, Japan, Canada and France. She has published novels, short story collections and books for children, including *Anger of Aubergines* (Kali for Women), *Banana Flower Dreams* (Penguin) and the *Fabled Book of Gods and Demons* (Puffin). Her books have been translated into Italian, French, German, Chinese, Spanish and Finnish.

She conducts storytelling and painting workshops for children with special needs.

Carmel Macdonald Grahame

Carmel Macdonald Grahame is a teacher of literature and creative writing. She holds a PhD in Australian literature and participates in community writing projects as an editor, workshop facilitator and mentor. Her work has appeared in literary journals and anthologies in Australia and Canada. Her novel, *Personal Effects*, was published with UWAP in 2014. She is a past winner of the Katharine Susannah Prichard Foundation Award for short fiction, the Patricia Hackett Prize for poetry and the Melbourne Poets Union Prize.

Carol Lefevre

Carol Lefevre holds a PhD in Creative Writing from the University of Adelaide, where she is a Visiting Research Fellow. Her most recent book *Murmurations,* a novella in eight stories (2020, Spinifex Press) was shortlisted for the 2021 Christina Stead Prize for Fiction in the NSW Premier's Literary Awards and the Adelaide Festival Awards. Her new book *The Tower* is a Spinifex Press publication (2022).

Cathie Koa Dunsford

Cathie Koa Dunsford is author of 26 books in print, including translations. She has performed at the Frankfurt, Leipzig and Istanbul book fairs and has toured globally with her translator, Karin Meissenburg, for 21 years. Spinifex Press published her Cowrie novel series featuring Indigenous lesbian characters.

Cheryl Adam

Cheryl Adam had her first novel *Lillian's Eden* published by Spinifex Press in 2018. *Out of Eden* followed in 2021 with the completion of the trilogy in 2022 with *Africa's Eden*. The novels draw on her experiences living and working in Europe and Africa and Eden in Australia. Cheryl was also a contributor to the 2021 non-fiction anthology *Not Dead Yet* published by Spinifex Press.

Coleen Clare

Coleen Clare claims Aotearoa as home although she now lives in Australia. Her short story examines the inner life of women living in a patriarchal world. Growing up between two brothers in a sexist home shaped her early conversion to feminism and social activism. She has a strong interest in social housing for older lesbians, working with Matrix Guild and WINC (Women in Co-housing). She enjoys observing the blossoming of a large extended family.

Colleen Higgs

Colleen Higgs is a writer, writing teacher, and publisher from Cape Town, South Africa. She is the author of two collections of poetry, *Halfborn Woman* (2004), and *Lava Lamp Poems* (2011) and a short story collection, *Looking for Trouble – Yeoville Stories* (2012). In 2020, her memoir, *my mother, my madness* was published to critical acclaim. She founded Modjaji Books in South Africa in 2007 and after publishing more than 150 books is still Modjaji's manager and publisher. She is also currently the coordinator of the English network of the International Alliance of Independent Publishers based in Paris.

Diane Bell

Diane Bell has been writing and telling stories for as long as she can remember. See Spinifex Press: *Daughters of the Dreaming* (1983, 2003), *Ngarrindjeri Wurruwarrin* (1998), *Radically Speaking* (1996) edited with Renate Klein, and *Evil: A Novel* (2005). Diane now lives on Ngunnawal country where she continues to write, plot and plan and imagine a better world while being Emerita Professor of Anthropology at the Australian National University and kayaking on the Molonglo River.

Fiona Place
Fiona Place is author of the prose poetry novel *Cardboard* (LCP, 1989, 2010) which won the National Book Council's Award for New Writers 1990 and non-fiction memoir *Portrait of the Artist's Mother: Dignity, Creativity and Disability* (Spinifex Press, 2019). Her book of poetry, *Corridor Offerings*, has been shortlisted for the Five Island Poetry Manuscript Prize 2022. She is currently working on a book of poetry, Fragments of a Life: Mothering a Child in Crisis.

Gena Corea
Gena Corea is the author of three books published by HarperCollins: *The Hidden Malpractice: How American Medicine Mistreats Women*; *The Invisible Epidemic* and *The Mother Machine*. With Janice Raymond, Corea is a co-founder of the National Coalition Against Surrogacy. She lives in Vermont, USA, where she is completing her book *Table in the Clearing: Stories of Sacred Jailbreaks*. For joy, Gena dances and drums in West African traditions.

Gina Mercer
Gina Mercer is a poet and book doula. She was Editor of *Island* from 2006 to 2010. She has published 11 books, including one novel, *Parachute Silk* (Spinifex Press, 2001) and seven poetry collections, her latest being *Watermark* (2022).

Jacque Duffy
Best known for her award-winning artworks, Jacque Duffy is an author and illustrator of books for children, articles, short

stories and poetry. She lives in the rainforests of Tropical North Queensland, Australia, where she is kept busy creating art and working on her first novel.

Jena Woodhouse

Jena Woodhouse is a Queensland-based author of 11 books and chapbooks, six of which are poetry titles. She lived and worked for a decade in Greece. Her interests include archaeology and mythology, as well as the natural world. Her writing has received awards for short and long fiction, children's fiction, and poetry.

Jordie Albiston

Jordie Albiston was a leading Australian poet who grew up in Melbourne. She studied music at the Victorian College of the Arts before completing a doctorate in English at La Trobe University. Her first book *Nervous Arcs,* was published by Spinifex Press in 1995. Another 19 books of poetry followed and she edited two others. She won many awards for her work including the Mary Gilmore Award and the Kenneth Slessor Prize for Poetry. In 2006, *The Hanging of Jean Lee* was staged as an opera at the Sydney Opera House. The libretto was shortlisted for the Victorian Premier's Prize for Best Music Theatre Script. Jordie received the Patrick White Literary Award in 2019 for her outstanding contribution to Australian literature. She was a finalist in the 2021 triennial career award, the Melbourne Prize for Literature. In 2022 she posthumously received the John Bray Poetry Award (South Australia) shortly after she died tragically in Melbourne at the age of 60. Two new volumes of poetry will be published in 2023.

Kerryn Higgs

Kerryn Higgs is the author of *All That False Instruction* (1975), Australia's first lesbian and our first second-wave feminist novel, re-published by Spinifex (2001). Her latest book, *Collision Course: Endless Growth on a Finite Planet* (MIT, 2014) tackles the ecological limits to economic growth. Kerryn is an environmental and feminist activist, an Associate Member of the Club of Rome, and founded the Mountain Collective. She has taught at Melbourne University and UNSW and mainly writes about the growth delusion and the often fictional quest for sustainability.

Laurie Ross Trott

Laurie Ross Trott grew up amidst Australia's northern rainforest. A journalist, she has worked in Sydney, Perth and regional Queensland. She was awarded First Class Honours in Screen Arts from Curtin University. Her poetry is published in print and online. Her play *To Kill A Cassowary* premiered in Cairns in 2020 and is published by Playlab Theatre. She lives at Mission Beach, where the Queensland Wet Tropics and Great Barrier Reef World Heritage areas meet.

Lizz Murphy

Lizz Murphy writes to feel connected. Born in Belfast, she now lives in Binalong in rural NSW. She has published 14 books including nine poetry titles. Her latest collection is *The Wear of My Face* (Spinifex Press), which won the 2021 Poetry (Big Press) section of the 2022 ACT Notable Awards. Her other Spinifex titles are *Two Lips Went Shopping* and the anthology *Wee Girls: Women Writing from an Irish Perspective*.

Lucy Sussex

Lucy Sussex is a New Zealand-born writer with a persistent interest in crime and women's history. Her award-winning work in various genres has been published internationally and in translation. She is an Honorary Fellow at La Trobe University, Bundoora.

Marion May Campbell

Marion May Campbell's recent works include the poetry collections *languish* (Upswell 2022) and *third body* (Whitmore Press 2018), and the memoir of her father *The Man on the Mantelpiece* (UWAP 2018). She lives in Drouin, on unceded GunaiKurnai land.

Marion Molteno

Marion Molteno is a prize-winning novelist and short story writer. She grew up in South Africa, but left because of her opposition to Apartheid. She lives in London. She has worked with multi-ethnic communities in the UK, and across Asia and Africa for Save the Children – experiences reflected in her latest book, *Journeys Without a Map: A Writer's Memoir.* < http://www.marionmolteno.co.uk>

Mary Goslett

Mary Goslett is a Saltwater woman of the Yuin nation and a contributor to *The Women's Pool* (Spinifex Press, 2021). She is also a mother, artist, clinical psychologist and consultant, living by the ocean.

Merlinda Bobis

Merlinda Bobis is an award-winning Filipina-Australian novelist, poet, and dramatist with 12 published books and ten performed works. She received the Christina Stead Prize and the Philippine National Book Award for her novel *Locust Girl, A Lovesong*, and the Canberra Critics' Circle Award for her latest book of short stories, *The Kindness of Birds,* which was shortlisted for the 2022 Christina Stead Prize and the Steele Rudd Award in the Queensland Literary Awards. She is Honorary Senior Lecturer at the Australian National University. <https://www.merlindabobis.com/>.

Patricia Sykes

Patricia Sykes is an award-winning poet and librettist. Her collaborations with composer Liza Lim have been performed in Australia, the UK, Germany, Moscow, Paris and New York. She was Asialink writer in Residence, Malaysia 2006. Her most recent collection is *Among the Gone of It*, English/Chinese, Flying Island Books, 2017. A song cycle by Andrew Aronowicz, based on her collection *The Abbotsford Mysteries* (Spinifex Press, 2011) premiered in May 2019. A podcast is forthcoming.

Pauline Hopkins

Pauline Hopkins is an editor at Spinifex Press and a bookseller. She lives on unceded Bunurong land.

Pramila Venkateswaran

Pramila Venkateswaran, poet laureate of Suffolk County, Long Island (2013-15) and co-director of Matwaala: South Asian Diaspora Poetry Festival, is the author of many poetry volumes, the most recent being *We are not a Museum* (Finishing Line Press, 2022). She has performed her poetry internationally, including at the Geraldine R. Dodge Poetry Festival. An award winning poet, she teaches English at SUNY, Nassau. She is the President of NOW, Suffolk, New York.

Renate Klein

Renate Klein feels deeply about the unethics of xeno-transplantation. She wants to know how many men give their organs to animals, especially pigs, and hopes for a world without cruel and heartless medicalisation. Among her recent books are *Surrogacy: A Human Rights Violation* (2017) and she is co-editor with Susan Hawthorne of *Not Dead Yet: Feminism, Passion and Women's Liberation* (2021).

Robyn Bishop

Robyn is a Melbourne based writer, actor and drama teacher. Her plays, two of which are published, have been performed at La Mama's Carlton Courthouse. Her debut novel *The Girl in the Bath* was published in 2014. She has recently completed a second novel and is working on a third, as well as a collection of short fiction. Robyn is passionate about telling Australian women's stories.

Sandy Jeffs

Sandy has published eight volumes of poetry and a memoir, *Flying with Paper Wings: Reflections on Living with Madness* (2009, 2016). She co-authored with Margaret Leggatt *Out of the Madhouse: From Asylums to Caring Community?* (2020). Sandy's most recent publication is *The Poetics of a Plague: A Haiku Diary* (Spinifex Press, 2021).

Sue Ingleton

Sue Ingleton is an award-winning actor, author, playwright, director and comedian. Dangerous teacher. Shamanic facilitator. Humourless Feminist. Disruptive grandmother. Owner builder. Working for Gaia. She is the author of *Making Trouble, Tongued with Fire: An Imagined History of Harriet Elphinstone Dick and Alice C. Moon* (Spinifex Press, 2019) and 11 plays.

Suniti Namjoshi

Suniti Namjoshi was born in Mumbai, India and lives in the southwest of England. Her books include *Feminist Fables* (1981, 1993), *Building Babel* (1996), *Saint Suniti and the Dragon* (1993), *Goja* (2000), *The Fabulous Feminist* (2012), *Suki* (2014), *Aesop the Fox* (2018) and *Dangerous Pursuits* (2022). Her children's books include the Aditi series, *The Boy and Dragon Stories* (2015) and *Blue and Other Stories* (2012).

Susan Hawthorne

Susan Hawthorne writes fiction, poetry and non-fiction and is the author and editor of 29 books. Among her latest books are *Vortex: The Crisis of Patriarchy* (2020), *The Sacking of the Muses* (2019) and *Dark Matters: A Novel* (2017). Her work has been published in many languages. She has had Literature Residencies in Chennai (2009), Rome (2013) and in Bursa (2018). She is Adjunct Professor at James Cook University, Townsville and the co-founder of Spinifex Press. She lives and works on Djiru Country.

Susan Midalia

Susan Midalia has published three short story collections, all shortlisted for major Australian literary awards: *A History of the Beanbag*, *An Unknown Sky* and *Feet to the Stars*. Her two novels are *The Art of Persuasion* and *Everyday Madness*. Her latest book is a collection of micro-fiction called *Miniatures*. She has a PhD in contemporary Australian women's fiction and has published on the subject in national and international literary journals. She has been a committed feminist since the 1970s, and has helped to raise two feminist adult sons.

Usha Akella

Usha Akella is a widely published poet whose work has featured in numerous literary journals. She has authored a number of poetry books including *I Will Not Bear You Sons* (Spinifex Press, 2021) as well as a chapbook, and has scripted two musical dramas. She earned a Master of Studies in Creative Writing from the University of Cambridge, UK and is the founder of Matwaala (www.matwaala.com) the first South Asian Diaspora Poets Festival in the US. She is the founder of the Poetry Caravan in New York and Austin, Texas, which takes poetry readings to the disadvantaged in women's shelters, senior homes, hospitals.

Acknowledgements

Thank you to the wonderful women who entrusted me with their stories and poems that form this anthology. Your talent and creativity astounds me and I am thrilled to be able to share your work with the world. Special thanks to Diane Bell for allowing us to use her story title as the book title.

I would like to express my deep gratitude to Susan Hawthorne and Renate Klein who have always been unwaveringly supportive and encouraging of me. You gave me my first opportunity in the world of publishing after I had been burned by politics, scarred by academia, and worked in diverse jobs across a range of fields. Not many people get to be lifeguards and editors in one lifetime! Your intellect, professionalism, insightful analysis and friendship guide and inspire me every day. Thank you sincerely, for everything.

This anthology would not have happened without the other amazing women in the Spinifex Press team: Maralann Damiano, Rachael McDiarmid, Caitlin Roper, Sharyn Murphy and Danielle Osborne. Thank you.

Thanks also to Helen Christie for her superb typesetting and to Deb Snibson for the beautiful cover design.

Heartfelt thanks to Carmel Bird, Gail Jones and Amanda Lohrey for your generous words of endorsement.

The time required to edit an anthology inevitably means that other things go by the wayside. Big hugs to my savvy daughter and fellow bookseller Piper for your input, advice and editing suggestions. Thanks to Bernie, for help in keeping things running and being head chef. Thanks to both of you for reminding me to chill, do the quiz and watch a movie sometimes.

I grew up in a house where books were treasured, words were important and education mattered. My dad was proud to have four feminist daughters and he would have been delighted to see this book in print. Thanks to my sisters Helen, Joanne and Savina, and my mum, Pinuccia, for sharing my love of words and for always being there.

Thank you to my dearest friends Bridget and Gisella to whom I can talk about anything.

Making room in my life for a dog when April, the most beloved dog of all, died suddenly at the start of the pandemic, has been a challenge. She is still on probation but the new dog Ruby has wheedled her way into our lives. Animals and the natural world have so much to teach us if we only take the time to listen and to appreciate that it is all connected. I'm still learning.

The Kindness of Birds

Merlinda Bobis

Shortlisted for the Christina Stead Prize for Fiction, the ACT Notable Awards and the Steele Rudd Award

An oriole sings to a dying father. A bleeding-heart dove saves the day. A crow wakes a woman's resolve. Owls help a boy endure isolation. Cockatoos attend the laying of the dead. Always there are birds in these linked stories that pay homage to kindness and the kinship among women and the planet. From Australia to the Philippines, across cultures and species, kindness inspires resilience amidst loss and grief.

ISBN 9781925950304

The Tower

Carol Lefevre

Widowed after a long marriage, Dorelia MacCraith swaps the family home for a house with a tower, and there, raised above the run of daily life, sets out to rewrite the stories of old women poorly treated by literature. The loneliness of not belonging, of being cut adrift by grief, betrayal, or old age, binds these twelve connected stories into a dazzling composite novel.

ISBN 9781925950625

Africa's Eden

Cheryl Adam

As a young unmarried mother in the 1960s, Maureen faces stifling disapproval from mainstream society. Desperate to create a new life, she rekindles an old romance and moves to South Africa under Apartheid. She finds death and despair, violence and injustice. But there is also humour, fun, family and friendship, as Maureen has to decide where her future lies. Is it Africa, or back home in Eden, in Australia?

ISBN 9781925950489

I Will Not Bear You Sons
Usha Akella

Usha Akella pays tribute to the lives of women from cultures across continents, while reflecting on her own life. Her poems are the medium for women who refuse to be silenced. She condenses a calm rage into ferocious words of precision and celebrates the women who have triumphed. All the while a subversive dusting of humour runs through this collection of poetry that cannot be ignored.

ISBN 9781925950281

An Embroidery of Old Maps and New
Angela Costi

Migration and the memories of women's traditions are woven throughout these poems. Angela Costi brings the world of Cyprus to Australia. Her mother encounters animosity on Melbourne's trams as Angela learns to thread words in ways that echo her grandmother's embroidery. Here are poems that sing their way across the seas and map histories.

ISBN 9781925950243

The Wear of My Face
Lizz Murphy

Winner, ACT Notable Awards (Poetry)

Here is an assemblage of passing lives and landscapes, fractured worlds and realities; splintered text and image, memory and dream, newscast and conversation. Women wicker first light, old men make things that glow, poets are standing stones, frontlines merge with tourist lines. Lizz Murphy weaves these elements into the strangeness of suburbia, the intensity of waiting rooms, and the stillness of the bush.

ISBN 9781925950342

Aesop the Fox
Suniti Namjoshi

Aesop's fables are brought to life by the timely intervention of Sprite from the future, who prods Aesop into debate about the meaning of stories: are they for fun, or do they have the chance to change the world? This book offers a virtuoso display into how the building blocks of fables can enchant, enrage, enlighten and educate us all.

ISBN 9781925581515

Making Trouble (Tongued with Fire): An Imagined History of Harriet Elphinstone Dick and Alice C. Moon
Sue Ingleton

In the cold winter of 1875, two rebellious spirits travel from the pale sunlight of England to the raw heat of Australia. Harriet Rowell and Alice Moon were champion swimmers in a time when women didn't go into the sea. In Australia, they achieve their freedom and create a path for others to follow, starting with opening a women's gymnasium. Harriet and Alice take on the world at a dangerous time for women's freedom of expression.

ISBN 9781925581713

Town of Love
Anne Ostby

They call them 'women of love,' but the lyrical beauty of the term has a hidden dark side: a workforce of very young girls tasked with feeding their families by offering up their bodies for sale. With insight and brutal honesty, Anne Ostby paints a vivid picture of some of the world's most vulnerable women and children. A raw and gripping story that is guaranteed to leave you breathless.

ISBN 9781742198477

The Poetics of a Plague
Sandy Jeffs

What was it like to live in Melbourne during the 2020 2.0 lockdown? Capturing the day-to-day struggles of lockdown, Sandy Jeffs takes us through the whirlwind of events in imaginative haiku poems. These became her sanity while the world spiralled into madness. Each day brings news that creates despair or joy. And as the world is in the grip of COVID madness, sanity is found in poetry.

ISBN 9781925950366

between wind and water (in a vulnerable place)
berni m janssen

between wind and water tells the stories of people who, after a windfarm is built in their neighbourhood, find that they begin to experience problems: sleep disruption, headaches, nausea, anxiety. They complain to the Company, local council, and government where they get lost in the labyrinth of doublespeak and duplicity, anxiety, disillusionment and a sense of abandonment grows.

ISBN 9781925581591

The Abbotsford Mysteries
Patricia Sykes

The Abbotsford Mysteries incorporates a medley of voices and experiences, drawn from official histories and other archives: the memories of Patricia and her sisters, and the oral memoirs of over 70 women, all who had been resident at the Good Shepherd Convent. The voices in these poems create multiple pathways through memory and time as they map and navigate the many-stranded mysteries of their institutionalised lives.

ISBN 9781876756956

Cowrie
Cathie Dunsford

Cowrie travels to Hawaii and, as she circles the island in an old pick-up truck, we discover the tokens of her heritage. Cowrie tests the limits of her endurance and explores her erotic connection with the earth. Island life erupts and you can taste the tropical fruit, the fish cooked in banana leaves and coconut, and smell the sweet fresh ginger.

ISBN 9781875559282

The Anger of Aubergines
Bulbul Sharma

Food as a passion, a gift, a means of revenge, even a source of power – these are the themes Bulbul Sharma explores in her entertaining collection of stories. Women weigh up the loss of a lover or the loss of weight; they consider whether hunger and the thought of higher things are inextricably linked; they feast and crave and die for their insatiable appetites.

ISBN 9781876756017

Portrait of the Artist's Mother:
Dignity, Creativity and Disability
Fiona Place

A memoir and an examination of the politics of disability, Fiona Place describes the pressure from medical institutions for screening and the assumptions about a child with Down syndrome. Her son Fraser has become a prize-winning artist. How does a mother get from the grieving silence of the birthing room to the applause at gallery openings? A story of courage, love and commitment to the idea that all people have a right to be welcomed into this increasingly imperfect world.

ISBN 9781925581751

All That False Instruction
Kerryn Higgs

A Spinifex feminist classic,
Winner of the Angus and Robertson manuscript prize

Growing up in a rural working-class home, Maureen rebels against her angry mother, the privileges of her favoured brother and the relentless conformity of 1950s Australia. University promises a new world both terrifying and exhilarating where Maureen explores her sexuality and makes a place for herself in the world. A funny and heartbreaking coming of age story.

ISBN 9781876756147

Parachute Silk: Friends, Food, Passion
A Novel in Letters
Gina Mercer

Molly and Finn are passionate friends who write to each other about lovers, risotto, mothering, and the many pleasures of the body, exchanging present intimacies and past secrets. Finn, at Molly's insistence, tells of her past love affairs in delicious detail. But there is one story that Finn cannot bear to tell. That is, until outside events force this secret from her.

ISBN 9781876756116

A Language in Common
Marion Molteno

A vivid collection of stories based on the author's nine years as an adult education worker among women from India and Pakistan living in Britain. With no common language, and in an often hostile and alien society, these women develop friendships across the boundaries of language and culture.

ISBN 9780958218603

The Body in Time/Nervous Arcs
Diane Fahey/Jordie Albiston

Winner, Mary Gilmore Award for Nervous Arcs
Runner-up, FAW Anne Elder Award for Nervous Arcs
Shortlisted, Kenneth Slessor Prize for Poetry for Nervous Arcs

Two poets known for delving into history and myth turn their attention to inner spaces, to time and the body's arcs. Jordie Albiston voices the unspoken languages of the body unearthing the complexity of memory, of desire and the art of the corporeal. Diane Fahey revisits the travelling body as it inhales memories of architecture and landscape. Scouring the body and the land for mines of trauma and of knowledge hard-won.

ISBN 9781875559374

Evil: A Novel
Diane Bell

The newly appointed professor, Dee P. Scrutari, turns her anthropological gaze on the tribe of non-reproducing males who dominate St Jude's, a prestigious Catholic liberal arts college. Evil is in the air. Something is awry. The determined anthropologist decodes the symbols and signs of evil as she teams up with a band of colleagues to solve a number of campus mysteries.

ISBN 9781876756550

Not Dead Yet: Feminism, Passion and Women's Liberation
Renate Klein and Susan Hawthorne (Editors)

Celebrating 30 years of feminist publishing by Spinifex Press, this latest joint volume by Renate Klein and Susan Hawthorne contains the accounts of 56 women, all 70 years of age or older, who share their experiences of the Women's Liberation Movement and their activism today. A riveting anthology about the struggle against patriarchy that will inspire and guide young women.

ISBN 9781925950328

*If you would like to know more about
Spinifex Press, write to us for a free catalogue, visit our
website or email us for further information
on how to subscribe to our monthly newsletter.*

Spinifex Press
PO Box 105
Mission Beach QLD 4852
Australia

www.spinifexpress.com.au
women@spinifexpress.com.au